MW00803761

Hansel and Gretel

Classic Collector's Series

Hansel and Gretel

and other stories by
THE BROTHERS GRIMM

Illustrated by
Kay Nielsen

WEATHERVANE BOOKS
New York

First published in 1925 by Hodder and Stoughton, England.

This 1985 edition published by Weathervane Books,
distributed by Crown Publishers, Inc.

ISBN 0517-491982

Manufactured in Spain.

D.L.B. 25359-1985

CONTENTS

CONTENTS

ILLUSTRATIONS

Facing page

ILLUSTRATIONS

Facing page

HANSEL AND GRETEL

NCE upon a time there dwelt near a large wood a poor woodcutter with his wife and two children by his former marriage, a little boy called Hansel, and a girl named Gretel. He had little enough to break or bite; and once, when there was a great famine in the land, he could not procure even his daily bread; and as he lay thinking in his bed one evening, rolling about for trouble, he sighed, and said to his wife, "What will become of us? How can we feed our children, when we have no more than we can eat ourselves?"

"Know then, my husband," answered she, "we will lead them away, quite early in the morning, into the thickest part of the wood, and there make them a fire, and give them each a little piece of bread; then we will go to our work, and leave them alone, so they will not find the way home again, and we shall be freed from them." "No, wife," replied he, "that I can never do; how can you bring your heart to leave my children all alone in the wood; for the wild beasts will soon come and tear them to pieces?"

"Oh, you simpleton!" said she, "then we must all four die of hunger; you had better plane the coffins for us." But she left him no peace till he consented, saying, "Ah, but I shall regret the poor children."

The two children, however, had not gone to sleep for very hunger, and so they overheard what the step-mother said to their father. Gretel wept bitterly, and said to Hansel, "What will become of us?" "Be quiet, Gretel," said he; "do not cry—I will soon help you." And as soon as their parents had fallen asleep, he got up, put on his coat, and, unbarring the back door, slipped out. The moon shone brightly, and the white pebbles which lay before the door seemed like silver pieces, they glittered so brightly. Hansel stooped down, and put as many into his pocket as it would hold; and then going back he said to Gretel, "Be comforted, dear sister, and sleep in peace; God will not forsake us." And so saying, he went to bed again.

The next morning, before the sun arose, the wife went and awoke the two children. "Get up, you lazy things; we are going into the forest to chop wood." Then she gave them each a piece of bread, saying, "There is something for your dinner; do not eat it before the time, for you will get nothing else." Gretel took the bread in her apron, for Hansel's pocket was full of pebbles; and so they all set out upon their way. When they had gone a little distance, Hansel stood still, and peeped back at the house; and this he repeated several times, till his father said, "Hansel, what are you peeping at, and why do you lag behind? Take care, and remember your legs."

"Ah, father," said Hansel, "I am looking at my white cat sitting upon the roof of the house, and trying to say good-bye." "You simpleton!" said the wife, "that is not a cat; it is only the sun shining on the white chimney." But in reality Hansel was not looking at a cat; but every time he stopped, he dropped a pebble out of his pocket upon the path.

When they came to the middle of the wood the father told the children to collect wood, and he would make them a fire, so that they should not be cold. So Hansel and Gretel gathered together quite a little mountain of twigs. Then they set fire to them; and as the flame burnt up high, the wife said, "Now, you children, lie down near the fire, and rest yourselves, whilst we go into the forest and chop wood; when we are ready I will come and call you."

Hansel and Gretel sat down by the fire, and when it was noon, each ate the piece of bread; and because they could hear the blows of an axe they thought their father was near: but it was not an axe, but a branch which he had bound to a withered tree so as to be blown to and fro by the wind. They waited so long that at last their eyes closed from weariness, and they fell fast asleep. When they awoke, it was quite dark, and Gretel began to cry, "How shall we get out of the wood?" But Hansel tried to comfort her by saying, "Wait a little while till the moon rises, and then we will quickly find the way." The moon soon shone forth, and Hansel, taking his sister's hand, followed the pebbles, which glittered like new-coined silver pieces, and showed them the path. All night long they walked on, and as day broke they came to their father's house. They knocked at the door, and when the wife opened it, and saw Hansel and Gretel, she exclaimed, "You wicked children! why did you sleep so long in the wood? We thought you were never coming home again." But their father was very glad, for it had grieved his heart to leave them all alone.

Not long afterwards there was again great scarcity in every corner of the land; and one night the children overheard their mother saying to their father, "Everything is again consumed; we have only half a loaf left, and then the song is ended: the children must be sent away. We will take them deeper into the wood, so that they may not find the way out again; it is the only means of escape for us."

But her husband felt heavy at heart, and thought, "It were better to share the last crust with the children." His wife, however, would listen to nothing that he said, and scolded and reproached him without end.

He who says A must say B too; and he who consents the first time must also the second.

The children, however, had heard the conversation as they lay awake, and as soon as the old people went to sleep Hansel got up, intending to pick up some pebbles as before; but the wife had locked the door, so that he could not get out. Nevertheless, he comforted Gretel, saying, "Do not cry; sleep in quiet; the good God will not forsake us."

Early in the morning the stepmother came and pulled them out of bed, and gave them each a slice of bread, which was still smaller than the former piece. On the way, Hansel broke his in his pocket, and, stooping every now and then, dropped a crumb upon the path. "Hansel, why do you stop and look about?" said the father, "keep in the path." "I am looking at my little dove," answered Hansel, "nodding a good-bye to me." "Simpleton!" said the wife, "that is no dove, but only the sun shining on the chimney." But Hansel kept still dropping crumbs as he went along.

The mother led the children deep into the wood, where they had never been before, and there making an immense fire, she said to them, "Sit down here and rest, and when you feel tired you can sleep for a little while. We are going into the forest to hew wood, and in the evening, when we are ready, we will come and fetch you."

When noon came Gretel shared her bread with Hansel, who had strewn his on the path. Then they went to sleep; but the evening arrived and no one came to visit the poor children, and in the dark night they awoke, and Hansel comforted his sister by saying, "Only wait, Gretel, till the moon comes out, then we shall see the crumbs of bread which I have dropped, and they will show us the way home." The moon shone and they got up, but they could not see any crumbs, for the thousands of birds which had been flying about in the woods and fields had picked them all up. Hansel kept saying to Gretel, "We will soon find the way"; but they did not, and they walked the whole night long and the next day, but still they did not come out of the wood; and they got so hungry, for they had nothing to eat but the berries which they found upon the bushes. Soon they got so tired that they could not drag themselves along, so they lay down under a tree and went to sleep.

It was now the third morning since they had left their father's house, and they still walked on; but they only got deeper and deeper into the wood, and Hansel saw that if help did not come very soon they would die of hunger. As soon as it was noon they saw a beautiful snow-white bird sitting upon a bough, which sang so sweetly that they stood still and listened to it. It soon left off, and spreading its wings flew off; and they followed it until it arrived at a cottage, upon the roof of which it perched; and when they went close up to it they saw that the cottage was made of bread and cakes, and the window-panes were of clear sugar.

"We will go in here," said Hansel, "and have a glorious feast. I will eat a piece of the roof, and you can eat the window. Will they not be sweet?" So Hansel reached up and broke a piece off the roof, in order to see how it tasted; while Gretel stepped up to the window and began to bite it. Then a sweet voice called out in the room, "Tip-tap, tip-tap, who raps at my door?" and the children answered, "The wind, the wind, the child of heaven!" and they went on eating without interruption. Hansel thought the roof tasted very nice, and so he tore off a great piece; while Gretel broke a large round pane out of the window, and sat down quite contentedly. Just then the door opened, and a very old woman, walking upon crutches, came out. Hansel and Gretel were so frightened that they let fall what they had in their hands; but the old woman, nodding her head, said, "Ah, you dear children, what has brought you here? Come in and stop with me, and no harm shall befall you!" and so saying she took them both by the hand, and led them into her cottage. A good meal of milk and pancakes, with sugar, apples, and nuts, was spread on the table, and in the back room were two nice little beds, covered with white, where Hansel and Gretel laid themselves down, and thought themselves in heaven. The old woman behaved very kindly to them, but in reality she was a wicked witch who waylaid children, and built the breadhouse in order to entice them in; but as soon as they were in her power she killed them, cooked and ate them, and made a great festival of the day. Witches have red eyes and cannot see very far; but they have a fine sense of smelling, like wild beasts, so that they know when children approach them. When Hansel and Gretel came near the witch's house she laughed wickedly, saying, "Here come two who shall not escape me." And early in the morning, before they awoke, she went up to them, and saw how lovingly they lay sleeping, with their chubby red cheeks; and she mumbled to herself, "That will be a good bite." Then she took up Hansel with her rough hand, and shut him up in a little cage with a lattice-door; and although he screamed loudly it was of no use. Gretel came next, and, shaking her till she awoke, she said, "Get up, you lazy thing, and fetch some water to cook something good for your brother, who must remain in that stall and get fat; when he is fat enough I shall eat him." Gretel began to cry, but it was all useless, for the old witch made her do as she wished. So a nice meal was cooked for Hansel, but Gretel got nothing else but a crab's claw.

Every morning the old witch came to the cage and said, "Hansel, stretch out your finger that I may feel whether you are getting fat." But Hansel used to stretch out a bone, and the old woman, having very bad sight, thought it was his finger, and wondered very much that he did not get more fat. When four weeks had passed, and Hansel still kept quite lean, she lost all her patience, and would not wait any longer. "Gretel," she called out in a passion, "get some water quickly; be Hansel fat or lean, this morning I will kill and cook him." Oh, how the poor little sister grieved, as she was forced to fetch the water, and fast the tears ran down her cheeks! "Dear good God, help us now!" she exclaimed. "Had we only been eaten by the wild beasts in the wood, then we should have died together." But the old witch called out, "Leave off that noise; it will not help you a bit."

So early in the morning Gretel was forced to go out and fill the kettle, and make a fire. "First, we will bake, however," said the old woman; "I have already heated the oven and kneaded the dough"; and so saying, she pushed poor Gretel up to the oven, out of which the flames were burning fiercely. "Creep in," said the witch, "and see if it is hot enough, and then we will put in the bread"; but she intended when Gretel got in to shut up the oven and let her bake, so that she might eat her as well as Hansel. Gretel perceived what her thoughts were, and said, "I do not know how to do it; how shall I get in?" "You stupid goose," said she, "the opening is big enough. See, I could even get in myself!" and she got up, and put her head into the oven. Then Gretel gave her a push, so that she fell right in, and then shutting the iron door she bolted it. Oh! how horribly she howled; but Gretel ran away and left the ungodly witch to burn to ashes.

Now she ran to Hansel, and, opening his door, called out, "Hansel, we are saved; the old witch is dead!" So he sprang out, like a bird out of his cage when the door is opened; and they were so glad that they fell upon each other's neck, and kissed each other over and over again. And now, as there was nothing to fear, they went into the witch's house, where in every corner were caskets full of pearls and precious stones. "These are better than pebbles," said Hansel, putting as many into his pocket as it would hold; while Gretel thought, "I will take some home too," and filled her apron full. "We must be off now," said Hansel, "and get out of this enchanted forest"; but when they had walked for two hours they came to a large piece of water. "We cannot get over," said Hansel; "I can see no bridge at all." "And there is no boat either," said Gretel; "but there swims a white duck, I will ask her to help us over"; and she sang:

"Little Duck, good little Duck,
Gretel and Hansel, here we stand;
There is neither stile nor bridge,
Take us on your back to land."

So the duck came to them, and Hansel sat himself on, and bade his sister sit behind him. "No," answered Gretel, "that will be too much for the duck, she shall take us over one at a time." This the good little bird did, and when both were happily arrived on the other side, and had gone a little way, they came to a well-known wood, which they knew the better every step they went, and at last they perceived their father's house. Then they began to run, and, bursting into the house, they fell on their father's neck. He had not had one happy hour since he had left the children in the forest: and his wife was dead. Gretel shook her apron, and the pearls and precious stones rolled out upon the floor, and Hansel threw down one handful after the other out of his pocket. Then all their sorrows were ended, and they lived together in great happiness.

THE SIX SWANS

KING was once hunting in a large wood, and pursued his game so hotly that none of his courtiers could follow him. But when evening approached he stopped, and looking around him perceived that he had lost himself. He sought a path out of the forest, but could not find one, and presently he saw an old woman with a nodding head, who came up to him. "My good woman," said he to her, "can you not show me the way out of the forest?"

"Oh, yes, my lord King," she replied; "I can do that very well, but upon one condition, which if you do not fulfil, you will never again get out of the wood, but will die of hunger."

"What, then, is this condition?" asked the King.

"I have a daughter," said the old woman, "who is as beautiful as any one you can find in the whole world, and well deserves to be your bride. Now, if you will make her your Queen, I will show you your way out of the wood." In the anxiety of his heart, the King consented, and the old woman led him to her cottage, where the daughter was sitting by the fire. She received the King as if she had expected him, and he saw at once that she was very beautiful, but yet she did not quite please him, for he could not look at her without a secret shuddering. However, after all he took the maiden upon his horse, and the old woman showed him the way, and the King arrived safely at his palace, where the wedding was to be celebrated.

The King had been married once before, and had seven children by his first wife, six boys and a girl, whom he loved above everything else in the world. He became afraid, soon, that the stepmother might not treat them very well, and might even do them some great injury, so he took them away to a lonely castle which stood in the midst of a forest. This castle was so hidden, and the way to it so difficult to discover, that he himself could not have found it if a wise woman had not given him a ball of cotton which had the wonderful property, when he threw it before him, of unrolling itself and showing him the right path. The King went, however, so often to see his dear children, that the Queen noticed his absence, became inquisitive, and wished to know what he went to fetch out of the forest. So she gave his servants a great quantity of money, and they disclosed to her the secret, and also told her of the ball of cotton which alone could show her the way. She had now no peace until she discovered where this ball was concealed, and then she made some fine silken shirts, and, as she had learnt of her mother, she sewed within each one a charm. One day soon after, when the King was gone out hunting, she took the little shirts and went into the forest, and the cotton showed her the path. The children, seeing some one coming in the distance, thought it was their dear father, and ran out towards her full of joy. Then she threw over each of them a shirt, which, as it touched their bodies, changed them into swans, which flew away over the forest. The Queen then went home quite contented and thought she was free of her stepchildren; but the little girl had not met her with the brothers, and the Queen did not know of her.

The following day the King went to visit his children, but he found only the maiden. "Where are your brothers?" asked he. "Ah, dear father," she replied, "they are gone away and have left me alone"; and she told him how she had looked out of the window and seen them changed into swans, which had flown over the forest; and then she showed him the feathers which they had dropped in the courtyard, and which she had collected together. The King was much grieved, but he did not think that his wife could have done this wicked deed, and, as he feared the girl might also be stolen away, he took her with him. She was, however, so much afraid of the stepmother, that she begged him not to stop more than one night in the castle.

The poor maiden thought to herself, "This is no longer my place, I will go and seek my brothers"; and when night came she escaped and went quite deep into the wood. She walked all night long and great part of the next day, until she could go no further from weariness. Just then she saw a rude hut, and walking in she found a room with six little beds, but she dared not get into one, but crept under, and, laying herself upon the hard earth, prepared to pass the night there. Just as the sun was setting, she heard a rustling, and saw six white swans come flying in at the window. They settled on the ground and began blowing one another until they had blown all their feathers off, and their swan's down stripped off like a shirt. Then the maiden knew them at once for her brothers, and gladly crept out from under the bed, and the brothers were not less glad to see their sister, but their joy was of short duration. "Here you must not stay," said they to her; "this is a robbers' hiding-place; if they should return and find you here, they will murder you." "Can you not protect me, then?" inquired the sister.

"No," they replied; "for we can only lay aside our swan's feathers for a quarter of an hour each evening, and for that time we regain our human form, but afterwards we resume our changed appearance."

Their sister then asked them with tears, "Can you not be restored again?"

"Oh, no," replied they, "the conditions are too difficult. For six long years you must neither speak nor laugh, and during that time you must sew together for us six little shirts of star-flowers, and should there fall a single word from your lips, then all your labour will be vain." Just as the brother finished speaking, the quarter of an hour elapsed, and they all flew out of the window again like swans.

The little sister, however, made a solemn resolution to rescue her brothers, or die in the attempt; and she left the cottage, and, penetrating deep into the forest, passed the night amid the branches of a tree. The next morning she went out and collected the star-flowers to sew together. She had no one to converse with, and for laughing she had no spirits, so there up in the tree she sat, intent upon her work. After she had passed some time there it happened that the King of that country was hunting in the forest, and his huntsmen came beneath the tree on which the maiden sat. They called to her and asked, "Who art thou?" But she gave no answer. "Come down to us," continued they: "we will do thee no harm." She simply shook her head, and, when they pressed her further with questions, she threw down to them her gold necklace, hoping therewith to satisfy them. They did not, however, leave her, and she threw down her girdle, but in vain; and even her rich dress did not make them desist. At last the hunter himself climbed the tree and brought down the maiden, and took her before the King. The King asked her, "Who art thou? What dost thou upon that tree?" But she did not answer; and then he asked her in all the languages that he knew, but she remained dumb to all as a fish. Since, however, she was so beautiful, the King's heart was touched, and he conceived for her a strong affection. Then he put around her his cloak, and, placing her before him on his horse, took her to his castle. There he ordered rich clothing to be made for her, and, although her beauty shone as the sunbeams, not a word escaped her. The King placed her by his side at table, and there her dignified mien and manners so won upon him, that he said, "This maiden will I marry, and no other in the world"; and after some days he was united to her.

Now, the King had a wicked stepmother, who was discontented with his marriage, and spoke evil of the young Queen. "Who knows whence the wench comes?" said she. "She who cannot speak is not worthy of a King." A year after, when the Queen brought her first-born into the world, the old woman took him away. Then she went to the King and complained that the Queen was a murderess. The King, however, would not believe it, and suffered no one to do any injury to his wife, who sat composedly sewing at her shirts and paying attention to nothing else. When a second child was born, the false stepmother used the same deceit, but the King again would

The little man dashed his right foot so deep
into the floor that he was forced to lay hold of
it with both hands to pull it out. (Page 242)

They saw that the cottage was made of bread
and cakes. (Page 8)

not listen to her words, but said, "She is too pious and good to act so: could she but speak and defend herself, her innocence would come to light." But when again, the third time, the old woman stole away the child, and then accused the Queen, who answered not a word to the accusation, the King was obliged to give her up to be tried, and she was condemned to suffer death by fire.

When the time had elapsed, and the sentence was to be carried out, it happened that the very day had come round when her dear brothers should be made free; the six shirts were also ready, all but the last, which yet wanted the left sleeve. As she was led to the scaffold, she placed the shirts upon her arm, and just as she had mounted it, and the fire was about to be kindled, she looked round, and saw six swans come flying through the air. Her heart leapt for joy as she perceived her deliverers approaching, and soon the swans, flying towards her, alighted so near that she was enabled to throw over them the shirts, and as soon as she had so done their feathers fell off and the brothers stood up alive and well; but the youngest wanted his left arm, instead of which he had a swan's wing. They embraced and kissed each other, and the Queen, going to the King, who was thunderstruck, began to say, "Now may I speak, my dear husband, and prove to you that I am innocent and falsely accused"; and then she told him how the wicked woman had stolen away and hidden her three children. When she had concluded, the King was overcome with joy, and the wicked stepmother was led to the scaffold and bound to the stake and burnt to ashes.

The King and the Queen for ever after lived in peace and prosperity with their six brothers.

LITTLE BROTHER AND LITTLE SISTER

HERE was once a little brother who took his sister by the hand, and said, "Since our own dear mother's death we have not had one happy hour; our stepmother beats us every day, and, if we come near her, kicks us away with her feet. Our food is the hard crusts of bread which are left, and even the dog under the table fares better than we, for he often gets a nice morsel. Come, let us wander forth into the wide world." So all day long they travelled over meadows, fields, and stony roads, and when it rained the sister said, "It is heaven crying in sympathy." By the evening they came into a large forest, and were so wearied with grief, hunger and their long walk, that they laid themselves down in a hollow tree, and went to sleep. When they awoke the next morning the sun had already risen high in the heavens, and its beams made the tree so hot that the little boy said to his sister, "I am so thirsty, if I knew where there was a brook I would go and drink. Ah! I think I hear one running"; and so saying, he got up, and taking his sister's hand, they went in search of the brook.

The wicked stepmother, however, was a witch, and had witnessed the departure of the two children; so, sneaking after them secretly, as is the habit of witches, she had enchanted all the springs in the forest.

Presently they found a brook, which ran trippingly over the pebbles, and the brother would have drunk out of it, but the sister heard how it said as it ran along, "Who drinks of me will become a tiger!" So the sister exclaimed, "I pray you, brother, drink not, or you will become a tiger, and tear me to pieces!" So the brother did not drink, although his thirst was so great, and he said, "I will wait till the next brook." As they came to the second, the sister heard it say, "Who drinks of me becomes a wolf!" The sister ran up crying, "Brother, do not, pray do not drink, or you will become a wolf and eat me up!" Then the brother did not drink, saying, "I will wait until we come to the next spring, but then I must drink, you may say what you will; my thirst is much too great." Just as they reached the third brook, the sister heard the voice saying, "Who drinks of me will become a fawn—who drinks of me will become a fawn!" So the sister said, "Oh, my brother! do not drink, or you will be changed to a fawn, and run away from me!" But he had already kneeled down, and drunk of the water, and, as the first drops passed his lips, his shape became that of a fawn.

At first the sister cried over her little changed brother,

and he wept too, and knelt by her very sorrowful; but at last the maiden said, "Be still, dear little fawn, and I will never forsake you"; and, undoing her golden garter, she put it round his neck, and weaving rushes made a white girdle to lead him with. This she tied to him, and taking the other end in her hand, she led him away, and they travelled deeper and deeper into the forest. After they had walked a long distance they came to a little hut, and the maiden, peeping in, found it empty, and thought, "Here we can stay and dwell." Then she looked for leaves and moss to make a soft couch for the fawn, and every morning she went out and collected roots and berries and nuts for herself, and tender grass for the fawn, which he ate out of her hand, and played happily around her. In the evening when the sister was tired, and had said her prayers, she laid her head upon the back of the fawn, which served for a pillow, on which she slept soundly. Had but the brother regained his own proper form, their life would have been happy indeed.

Thus they dwelt in this wilderness, and some time had elapsed when it happened that the King of the country held a great hunt in the forest; and now resounded through the trees the blowing of horns, the barking of dogs, and the lusty cries of the hunters, so that the little fawn heard them, and wanted very much to join. "Ah!" said he to his sister, "let me go to the hunt, I cannot restrain myself any longer" ; and he begged so hard that at last she consented. "But," said she to him, "return again in the evening, for I shall shut my door against the wild huntsmen, and, that I may know you, do you knock, and say, 'Sister, let me in,' and if you do not speak I shall not open the door." As soon as she had said this, the little fawn sprang off quite glad and merry in the fresh breeze. The King and his huntsmen perceived the beautiful animal, and pursued him; but they could not catch him, and when they thought they had him for certain, he sprang away over the bushes and got out of sight. Just as it was getting dark, he ran up to the hut, and, knocking, said, "Sister mine, let me in." Then she undid the little door, and he went in, and rested all night long upon his soft couch. The next morning the hunt was commenced again, and as soon as the little fawn heard the horns and the tally-ho of the sportsmen he could not rest, and said, "Sister, dear, open the door, I must be off." The sister opened it, saying, "Return at evening, mind, and say the words as before." When the King and his huntsmen saw again the fawn with the golden necklace, they followed him close, but he was too nimble and quick for them. The whole day long they kept up with him, but towards evening the huntsmen made a circle round him, and one wounded him slightly in the foot behind, so that he could only run slowly. Then one of them slipped after him to the little hut, and heard him say, "Sister, dear, open the door," and saw that the door was opened and immediately shut behind. The huntsman, having observed all this, went and told the King what he had seen and heard, and he said, "On the morrow I will once more pursue him."

The sister, however, was terribly frightened when she saw that her fawn was wounded, and, washing off the blood, she put herbs upon the foot, and said, "Go and rest upon your bed, dear fawn, that the wound may heal." It was so slight, that the next morning he felt nothing of it, and when he heard the hunting cries outside, he exclaimed, "I cannot stop away—I must be there, and none shall catch me so easily again!" The sister wept very much, and told him, "Soon they will kill you, and I shall be here all alone in this forest, forsaken by all the world: I cannot let you go."

"I shall die here in vexation," answered the fawn, "if you do not, for when I hear the horn I think I shall jump out of my skin." The sister, finding she could not prevent him, opened the door with a heavy heart, and the fawn jumped out, quite delighted, into the forest. As soon as the King perceived him, he said to his huntsmen, "Follow him all day long to the evening, but let no one do him an injury." When the sun had set, the King asked his huntsmen to show him the hut; and as they came to it, he knocked at the door, and said, "Let me in, dear sister." Then the door was opened, and stepping in, the King saw a maiden more beautiful than he had ever before seen. She was frightened when she saw not her fawn, but a man step in, who had a golden crown upon his head. But the King, looking at her with a friendly glance, reached her his hand, saying, "Will you go with me to my castle, and be my dear wife?" "Oh, yes," replied the maiden; "but the fawn must go too: him I will never forsake." The King replied, "He shall remain with you as long as you live, and shall want for nothing." In the meantime the fawn had come in, and the sister, binding the girdle to him, again took it in her hand, and led him away with her out of the hut.

The King took the beautiful maiden upon his horse, and rode to his castle, where the wedding was celebrated with great splendour, and she became Queen, and they lived together a long time; while the fawn was taken care of and lived well, playing about the castle garden. The wicked stepmother, however, on whose account the children had wandered forth into the world, supposed that long ago the sister had been torn in pieces by the wild beasts, and the little brother hunted to death in his fawn's shape by the hunters. As soon, therefore, as she heard how happy they had become, and how everything prospered with them, envy and jealousy were roused in her heart, and left her no peace; and she was always thinking in what way she could work misfortune to them. Her own daughter, who was as ugly as night, and had but one eye, for which she was continually reproached, said, "The luck of being a Queen has never yet happened to me." "Be quiet now," said the old woman, "and make yourself contented: when the time comes, I shall be at hand." As soon, then, as the time came when the Queen brought into the world a beautiful little boy, which happened when the King was out hunting, the old witch took the form of a chambermaid, and got into the room where the Queen was lying, and said to her, "The bath is ready, which will restore you and give you fresh strength; be quick, before it gets cold." Her daughter being at hand, they carried the weak Queen between them into the room, and laid her in the bath, and then, shutting the door to, they ran off; but first they made up an immense fire in the stove, which must soon suffocate the young Queen.

When this was done, the old woman took her daughter, and, putting a cap on her, laid her in the bed in the Queen's place. She gave her, too, the form and appearance of the real Queen, as far as she could; but she could not restore the lost eye, and, so that the King might not notice it, she turned upon that side where there was no eye. When he came home at evening, and heard that a son was born to him, he was much delighted, and prepared to go to his wife's bedside, to see how she did. So the old woman called out in a great hurry, "For your life, do not undraw the curtains; the Queen must not yet see the light, and must be kept quiet." So the King went away, and did not discover that a false Queen was laid in the bed.

When midnight came, and every one was asleep, the nurse, who sat by herself wide awake, near the cradle, in the nursery, saw the door open and the true Queen come in. She took the child in her arms, and rocked it a while, and then, shaking up its pillow, laid it down, in its cradle, and covered it over again. She did not forget the fawn either, but, going to the corner where he was, stroked his back, and then went silently out of the door. The nurse asked in the morning of the guards if any one had passed into the castle during the night; but they answered, "No, we have seen nobody." For many nights afterwards she came constantly, and never spoke a word; and the nurse saw her always but she would not trust herself to speak about it to any one.

When some time had passed away, the Queen one night began to speak, and said:

> "How fares my child, how fares my fawn?
> Twice more will I come, but never again."

The nurse made no reply; but, when she had disappeared, went to the King, and told him all. The King exclaimed, "Oh, heavens! what does this mean?—the next night I will watch myself by the child." In the evening he went into the nursery and about midnight the Queen appeared, and said:

" How fares my child, how fares my fawn ?
Once more will I come, but never again."

And she nursed the child, as she was used to do, and then disappeared. The King dared not speak; but he watched the following night, and this time she said:

" How fares my child, how fares my fawn ?
This time have I come, but never again."

At these words the King could hold back no longer, but sprang up and said, " You can be no other than my dear wife ! " Then she answered, " Yes, I am your dear wife " ; and at that moment her life was restored by God's mercy, and she was again as beautiful and charming as ever. She told the King the fraud which the witch and her daughter had practised upon him, and he had them both tried and sentence pronounced against them. The daughter was taken into the forest, where the wild beasts tore her in pieces, but the old witch was led to the fire and miserably burnt. As soon as she was reduced to ashes the little fawn was unbewitched, and received again his human form; and the brother and sister lived happily together to the end of their days.

When she had concluded, the King
was overcome with joy. (Page 24)

Then the fisherman went home and found his wife sitting upon a throne, and she had three great crowns upon her head. (Page 47)

THE FISHERMAN AND HIS WIFE

HERE was once a fisherman who lived with his wife in a ditch, close by the seaside. The fisherman used to go out all day long a-fishing; and one day, as he sat on the shore with his rod, looking at the shining water and watching his line, all on a sudden his float was dragged away deep under the sea: and in drawing it up he pulled a great fish out of the water. The fish said to him, "Pray let me live: I am not a real fish, I am an enchanted Prince; put me in the water again, and let me go." "Oh!" said the man, "you need not make so many words about the matter; I wish to have nothing to do with a fish that can talk; so swim away as soon as you please." Then he put him back into the water, and the fish darted straight down to the bottom, and left a long streak of blood behind him.

When the fisherman went home to his wife in the ditch, he told her how he had caught a great fish, and how it had told him it was an enchanted Prince, and that on hearing it speak he had let it go again. "Did you not ask it for anything?" said the wife. "No," said the man, "what should I ask for?" "Ah!" said the wife, "we live very wretchedly here in this nasty stinking ditch; do go back, and tell the fish we want a little cottage."

The fisherman did not much like the business: however, he went to the sea, and when he came there the water looked all yellow and green. And he stood at the water's edge, and said:

> "O man of the sea!
> Come listen to me,
> For Alice my wife,
> The plague of my life,
> Hath sent me to beg a boon of thee!"

Then the fish came swimming to him, and said, "Well, what does she want?" "Ah!" answered the fisherman, "my wife says that when I had caught you, I ought to have asked you for something before I let you go again; she does not like living any longer in the ditch, and wants a little cottage." "Go home, then," said the fish, "she is in the cottage already." So the man went home, and saw his wife standing at the door of a cottage. "Come in, come in," said she; "is not this much better than the ditch?" And there was a parlour, and a bed-chamber, and a kitchen; and behind the cottage there was a little garden with all sorts of flowers and fruits, and a courtyard full of ducks and chickens. "Ah!" said the fisherman, "how happily we shall live!" "We will try to do so, at least," said his wife.

Everything went right for a week or two, and then Dame Alice said, " Husband, there is not room enough in this cottage, the courtyard and garden are a great deal too small; I should like to have a large stone castle to live in; so go to the fish again, and tell him to give us a castle." " Wife," said the fisherman, " I don't like to go to him again, for perhaps he will be angry; we ought to be content with the cottage." " Nonsense! " said the wife; " he will do it very willingly; go along, and try."

The fisherman went; but his heart was very heavy: and when he came to the sea, it looked blue and gloomy, though it was quite calm. And he went close to it, and said:

" O man of the sea !
Come listen to me,
For Alice my wife,
The plague of my life,
Hath sent me to beg a boon of thee ! "

" Well, what does she want now? " said the fish. " Ah! " said the man very sorrowfully, " my wife wants to live in a stone castle." " Go home, then," said the fish, " she is standing at the door of it already." So away went the fisherman, and found his wife standing before a great castle. " See," said she, " is not this grand? " With that they went into the castle together, and found a great many servants there, and the rooms all richly furnished and full of golden chairs and tables; and behind the castle was a garden, and a wood half a mile long, full of sheep, and goats, and hares, and deer; and in the courtyard were stables and cow-houses. "Well," said the man, "now will we live contented and happy in this beautiful castle for the rest of our lives." "Perhaps we may," said the wife; "but let us consider and sleep upon it before we make up our minds": so they went to bed.

The next morning, when Dame Alice awoke, it was broad daylight, and she jogged the fisherman with her elbow, and said, "Get up, husband, and bestir yourself, for we must be king of all the land." "Wife, wife," said the man, "why should we wish to be king? I will not be king." "Then I will," said Alice. "But, wife," answered the fisherman, "how can you be king? the fish cannot make you a king." "Husband," said she, "say no more about it, but go and try; I will be king!" So the man went away, quite sorrowful to think that his wife should want to be king. The sea looked a dark grey colour, and was covered with foam as he cried out:

"O man of the sea!
Come listen to me,
For Alice my wife,
The plague of my life,
Hath sent me to beg a boon of thee!"

"Well, what would she have now?" said the fish. "Alas!" said the man, "my wife wants to be king." "Go home," said the fish; "she is king already."

Then the fisherman went home; and as he came close to the palace, he saw a troop of soldiers, and heard the sound of drums and trumpets; and when he entered in, he saw his wife sitting on a high throne of gold and diamonds, with a golden crown upon her head; and on each side of her stood six beautiful maidens, each a head taller than the other. "Well, wife," said the fisherman, "are you king?" "Yes," said she, "I am king." And when he had looked at her for a long time, he said, "Ah, wife! what a fine thing it is to be king! now we shall never have anything more to wish for." "I don't know how that may be," said she; "never is a long time. I am king, 'tis true, but I begin to be tired of it, and I think I should like to be emperor." "Alas, wife! why should you wish to be emperor?" said the fisherman. "Husband," said she, "go to the fish; I say I will be emperor." "Ah, wife!" replied the fisherman, "the fish cannot make an emperor, and I should not like to ask for such a thing." "I am king," said Alice, "and you are my slave, so go directly!" So the fisherman was obliged to go; and he muttered as he went along, "This will come to no good, it is too much to ask; the fish will be tired at last, and then we shall repent of what we have done." He soon arrived at the sea, and the water was quite black and muddy, and a mighty whirlwind blew over it; but he went to the shore, and said:

"O man of the sea!
Come listen to me,
For Alice my wife,
The plague of my life,
Hath sent me to beg a boon of thee!"

"What would she have now!" said the fish. "Ah!" said the fisherman, "she wants to be emperor." "Go home," said the fish; "she is emperor already."

So he went home again; and as he came near he saw his wife sitting on a very lofty throne made of solid gold, with a great crown on her head full two yards high, and on each side of her stood her guards and attendants in a row, each one smaller than the other, from the tallest giant down to a little dwarf no bigger than my finger. And before her stood princes, and dukes, and earls: and the fisherman went up to her and said, "Wife, are you emperor?" "Yes," said she, "I am emperor." "Ah!" said the man as he gazed upon her, "what a fine thing it is to be emperor!" "Husband," said she, "why should we stay at being emperor; I will be pope next." "O wife, wife!" said he, "how can you be pope? there is but one pope at a time in Christendom." "Husband," said she, "I will be pope this very day." "But," replied the husband, "the fish cannot make you pope." "What nonsense!" said she, "if he can make an emperor, he can make a pope; go and try him." So the fisherman went. But when he came to the shore the wind was raging, and the sea was tossed up and down like boiling water, and the ships were in the greatest distress and danced upon the waves most fearfully; in the middle of the sky there was a little blue, but towards the south it was all red as if a dreadful storm was rising. At this the fisherman was terribly frightened, and trembled, so that his knees knocked together: but he went to the shore and said:

" O man of the sea !
Come listen to me,
For Alice my wife,
The plague of my life,
Hath sent me to beg a boon of thee ! "

"What does she want now?" said the fish. "Ah!" said the fisherman, " my wife wants to be pope." " Go home," said the fish, " she is pope already."

Then the fisherman went home, and found his wife sitting on a throne that was two miles high; and she had three great crowns on her head, and around stood all the pomp and power of the Church; and on each side were two rows of burning lights, of all sizes, the greatest as large as the highest and biggest tower in the world, and the least no larger than a small rushlight. " Wife," said the fisherman as he looked at all this grandeur, " are you pope?" "Yes," said she, " I am pope." " Well, wife," replied he, " it is a grand thing to be pope; and now you must be content, for you can be nothing greater." " I will consider of that," said the wife. Then they went to bed: but Dame Alice could not sleep all night for thinking what she should be next. At last morning came, and the sun rose. "Ha!" thought she as she looked at it through the window, "cannot I prevent the sun rising?" At this she was very angry, and she wakened her husband, and said, "Husband, go to the fish and tell him I want to be lord of the sun and moon." The fisherman was half asleep, but the thought frightened him so much, that he started and fell out of bed. "Alas, wife!" said he, "cannot you be content to be pope?" "No," said she, "I am very uneasy, and cannot bear to see the sun and moon rise without my leave. Go to the fish directly."

Then the man went trembling for fear; and as he was going down to the shore a dreadful storm arose, so that the trees and the rocks shook; and the heavens became black, and the lightning played, and the thunder rolled; and you might have seen in the sea great black waves like mountains with a white crown of foam upon them; and the fisherman said:

"O man of the sea!
Come listen to me,
For Alice my wife,
The plague of my life,
Hath sent me to beg a boon of thee!"

"What does she want now?" said the fish. "Ah!" said he, "she wants to be lord of the sun and moon." "Go home," said the fish, "to your ditch again!" And there they live to this very day.

THE DRUMMER

NE evening a young Drummer was walking by himself in the fields. He came to a lake, where he found on the bank three little bits of white linen. "This is very fine linen," he said, and put a bit in his pocket. He then went home, and without thinking any more about his find, lay down in bed.

Just as he was composing himself to sleep he fancied some one called his name. He listened, and then a low voice fell distinctly on his ear.

"Drummer, drummer, wake up!" it said.

The night was so dark that he could see no one, but he felt as if a figure were floating up and down at the bottom of his bed. "What do you want?" he asked.

"Give me back my garment that you took away last night from the shore."

"You shall have it," answered the Drummer, "if you tell me who you are."

"Ah!" said the voice, "I am the daughter of a mighty King, but I am in the power of a witch, and I am banished to the glass mountain. Every day I have to bathe in the lake with my two sisters, but without my garment I can't fly away again. My sisters have flown off long ago, but I am obliged to stay behind. I implore you to give it back to me."

"Be calm, child," said the Drummer. "I will give it to you, of course."

He went and took the linen out of his pocket and handed it to her. She seized it eagerly, and turned to go.

"Wait a minute," said he, "perhaps I can help you."

"You can only help me," she replied, "by mounting the glass mountain and delivering me out of the hands of the witch. But you couldn't possibly do it; even if you were quite close to the mountain you couldn't climb it."

"Where there is a will, there's a way," said the Drummer. "I pity you, and fear nothing. But I don't know the way to the glass mountain."

"The path lies through a forest inhabited by cannibals; that is all I may tell you," she answered. And then he heard her flit away.

At daybreak the Drummer got up, slung on his drum, and went fearlessly into the cannibal forest. After he had gone a little distance he looked round, but saw no giants. He thought, "I must wake up the sluggards," and he beat a tattoo on his drum which frightened the birds.

In a few minutes a giant who had been lying in the grass reared his huge form, and stood there as tall as a pine-tree. "You rascal!" he exclaimed, "what do you mean by beating your drum and waking me out of my beauty sleep?"

"I am beating the drum," he answered, "because a thousand men are coming behind who want to know the way."

"What are they doing in my forest?" asked the giant.

"They intend, for one thing, to kill you, and cleanse the forest from all such monsters."

"Oh, indeed," said the giant. "I'll trample them dead like so many ants."

"Do you think you could catch them?" said the Drummer, with a sneer. "If you stooped to pick up one he would be off like a shot and hide himself, and if you lay down to sleep hundreds would creep out of the bushes and climb on your body; and as they are all armed with steel hammers they would make short work of beating in your skull."

The giant grew sad, and thought: "It is difficult to know how to deal with these small, cunning folk. With wolves and bears I am at home, but I am at a loss what to do with earth-worms."

"Look here," he said aloud, "if you, little fellow, will go away now, I promise I will never molest you and your comrades in future, and if you have any particular wish that I can fulfil, tell me, and I will see what I can do for you."

"You have long legs," said the Drummer, "and can run faster than I. Carry me to the glass mountain, and I will signal to my men to retreat and leave you in peace."

"Come here then, little worm," said the giant, "seat yourself on my shoulder, and I will carry you wherever you want to go."

The giant lifted him, and the Drummer began to play his drum from sheer joy. The giant thought this was the signal for the others to withdraw.

After a time a second giant stood in the path, who took the Drummer away from the first giant and put him in his button-hole. The Drummer held on to the button, which was as big as a dish, and still felt in quite good spirits.

Then they came to a third giant, who took the Drummer out of the other's button-hole, and put him on the brim of his hat. The Drummer walked up and down, and could see away over the tree-tops. Catching sight of a mountain in the blue distance, he thought to himself, "That is the glass mountain for certain," and it was. The giant had only to take a few strides to get to the foot of it.

When the giant put him down, the Drummer desired him to carry him to the top, but the giant muttered something in his beard, and went back to the forest.

K·N

There stood the poor Drummer in front of the mountain that was so high; it was like three ordinary mountains, one on top of the other, and as transparent and smooth, besides, as a mirror. He did not know what to do. He tried to climb, but in vain, for he always tumbled back.

As he stood there, not knowing how he should act, he caught sight of two men fighting. He went up to them, and saw that the bone of contention was a saddle lying on the ground.

"What fools you are," he said, "to quarrel about a saddle when you have no horse to put it on."

"The saddle is worth quarrelling about," replied one of the men. "If any one sits on it, and wishes himself somewhere, even at the end of the world, he'll be there in a jiffy. The saddle is our joint property. It is my turn to ride on it, but he will not let me."

"I will settle the dispute," said the Drummer. He went a few paces off and stuck a white pole into the ground. Then he came back, and said, "Now then, run to the pole, and who reaches it first will have first right to the saddle."

Both started, but they had not run many steps before the Drummer swung himself into the saddle and wished himself at the top of the glass mountain. In a twinkling he was there.

An old stone house stood on the very top, in front of which was a large fishpond, and beneath it a dense, dark wood. He did not see a sign of man or beast. All was silent except for the rustling of the trees. The clouds seemed very close over his head.

He knocked at the door of the house, but not till he had knocked three times did an old woman with a brown face and pink eyes open it. She had spectacles on her long nose, and scanned him sharply. Then she asked what his business was, and he asked for board and lodging. "You shall have it," replied the old lady, "if you work for it. I will set you three tasks."

"Why not?" said the Drummer. "I don't shirk work, and I don't care how hard it is."

The old woman then admitted him, giving him a good supper and a comfortable bed.

In the morning she took a thimble from her shrivelled finger, and, handing it to the Drummer, said: "Take this thimble and with it bale out the water in the pond till there isn't a drop left. The work must be completed by night, and all the fish arranged according to their kind and size on the bank."

"A curious task," thought the Drummer. He went to the pond and began to bale. He worked hard the whole morning, but what was the good of trying to empty a great sheet of water with a thimble? It would take a thousand years at least. At dinner-time he gave it up as a bad job, saying to himself, "It is all the same whether I work or not."

Then a maiden came out of the house and placed a basket of food before him. "How sad you seem!" she said. "Is anything the matter?"

He looked at her and saw she was very beautiful. "Alas!" he exclaimed, "I cannot perform the first task she has given me. How shall I ever be able to perform the other two? I came here to seek a Princess, but I have not seen her yet."

"Wait here," said the girl; "I will help you. You are tired; lay your head in my lap and sleep, and when you wake the thing will be done."

The Drummer was only too charmed to obey.

Directly his eyes closed the girl twisted a wishing-ring, and exclaimed, "Water, come up. Fish, come out."

The water immediately rose like a white mist and mingled with the other clouds, and the fish jumped on to the bank and arranged themselves in order of size and colour.

When the Drummer awoke he saw with amazement what had happened.

The girl said, "One of the fish is not lying by his fellows, but is quite alone. If the old woman comes this evening to see if all has been done as she ordered, she will at once say, 'What is this fish doing here?' Then throw the fish in her face, and say, 'It is for you, old witch.'"

At evening, when the old woman came and asked

the question, he threw the fish in her face. She stood as if she did not notice the insult and said nothing, but her eyes blinked wickedly.

The next morning she remarked, " Yesterday you had too easy a time; I must give you harder work. To-day you must cut down the whole wood, cut up the timber, arrange it into faggots, and everything must be ready by the evening." She gave him an axe, a hatchet, and two saws, but they were all made of lead.

He did not know what to do, but the maiden arrived at dinner-time with his food, and said, " Lay your head in my lap, go to sleep, and when you wake the work will be finished."

She twisted her wish-ring on her finger, and the whole wood collapsed with one fearful crackle, as if invisible giants had been felling it.

He awoke, and the girl said, " Look! the timber is all severed and arranged in faggots. Only one branch lies apart; when the old woman comes to-night, take it and give her a blow with it, and say, 'That 's for you, old witch.' "

The old woman came. " You see," she said, " how very easy is the work I give you. But what is that branch doing there? "

He took it up and gave her a bang with it, saying, " That 's for you, old witch." But she appeared not to feel it, and only laughed mockingly.

"To-morrow," she said, "you shall collect all the faggots, pile them up, and set fire to them."

He rose at dawn and began to collect the wood, but how was it possible for a single man to gather a whole forest? He made no progress. Well for him that the girl did not leave him in the lurch! She brought his dinner, and when he had eaten it he put his head in her lap and went to sleep. On waking, the whole vast mass of timber was alight, the flames reaching to the sky.

"Listen," said the girl, "when the witch comes she will impose on you again. Do what she asks you without fear, so that you give her no cause for complaint. If you are the least bit afraid, she will seize you and pitch you into the furnace. When you have done as she bids you, you can end by catching hold of her and throwing *her* on the flames."

The girl departed, and the old witch came. "Fire! I am freezing!" she exclaimed, "but that nice fire will warm my old bones. But look, there's a log that won't burn; fetch it out. If you can do that, you are free to wander where you please, so jump in gaily."

The Drummer did not hesitate a moment and sprang into the flames; they did not even singe his hair. He dragged out the log and laid it down. Hardly had it touched the earth than it changed into the charming girl who had helped him out of his difficulties, and by the golden draperies she now wore he knew she was the Princess.

The old woman laughed. "You think," she jeered, "that you've got her, but I tell you, you haven't yet."

She was in the act of rushing at the girl to take her away, when the Drummer seized the old woman with both hands and flung her into the fire.

The Princess then looked critically at the Drummer, and having duly considered that he was certainly a handsome youth who had risked his life for her sake, she held out her hand, and said, "You have dared everything for me. Promise to be my true love, and I will marry you."

She led him into the house and showed him great chests and cupboards, filled with the treasures the witch had accumulated. They left all the gold and silver and only took the precious stones.

As they did not wish to linger on the glass mountain any longer, she said to him, "I have only to turn my wishing-ring and we shall be at home."

"All right," said the Drummer, "wish us in front of the city gates."

In a second they were there, and the Drummer said, "First I will go to my parents and tell them the news. Wait for me here in this field and I will soon be back."

"Ah!" cried the Princess, "I implore you to be careful. On no account kiss your parents on the right cheek, else you will forget everything."

"How could I possibly forget you?" he said, and gave her his right hand and promised that he would soon return.

When he entered his old home no one knew him, he was so altered, for the three days he had spent on the glass mountain had really been three years.

Then he revealed who he was, and his parents in their delight fell on his neck, and he was so touched that he kissed them on both cheeks, forgetting the maiden's injunction. Directly he had kissed the right cheeks of his parents all thought of the Princess left him. He emptied his pockets, and laid handfuls of pearls and diamonds on the table. The parents did not know what to do with all this wealth.

At last the father built a superb castle, surrounded by gardens, fields and woods, fit for a prince to live in. And when it was ready the mother said to the Drummer, "I have chosen a bride for you, and we will fix the wedding for this day week." The son expressed himself content.

The poor Princess meanwhile had waited a long time in the field before the city gates. When evening came, and he did not return, she felt convinced that he had kissed his parents on the right cheek and forgotten all about her. Her heart was heavy, and she wished herself in a lonely forest house and not at her father's court. Every evening she walked into the town and passed the Drummer's house; many times the youth saw her without knowing her again. At last she heard people saying,

"To-morrow he is to be married." And she thought, "I will make an effort to win him back."

On the first day of the wedding festivities she twirled her ring, and said, "I want a dress that shines like the sun." At once the garment lay before her, and looked as if it had been woven out of sunbeams.

When the guests were assembled she entered the hall. Every one was struck by the beauty of her dress, especially the bride herself, who had a passion for fine clothes. She went up to the stranger and asked if she would sell her gown.

"Not for money," was the answer, "but if I may linger all night beside the door of the room in which the bridegroom is going to sleep, I will give you the dress with pleasure."

The bride could not resist the offer, and consented to the arrangement, but first she mixed the bridegroom a sleeping-draught with his wine, which sent him into a deep slumber.

When the house was quiet the Princess crouched before the door of the sleeping apartment, opened it a little, and called:

> "Drummer, drummer, listen to me.
> Have you forgotten me quite?
> Did you not sit beside me on the mountain height?
> Did I not save you from the witch's wiles?
> And you plighted your troth with smiles?
> Drummer, drummer, listen to me."

But it was no use; the Drummer did not wake, and when morning dawned the Princess was obliged to own herself unsuccessful and go away.

The second evening she turned her ring, and said, "I want a dress as silver as the moon."

When she appeared in draperies as soft and filmy as moonbeams, she again excited the envy of the bride, who accepted the dress as a present and granted the wearer permission to spend another night outside the bridegroom's door.

In the stillness of the night she called again to the Drummer, but as he was stupefied by the sleeping-draught he did not waken, and in the morning the Princess went sorrowfully back to her forest house.

But some of the servants in the house had heard the strange girl's sad lament and told the bridegroom about it; they told him that he must have heard it if he had not been drugged with the sleeping-draught that had been mixed with his night-cap.

The third evening the Princess turned her ring, and said, "I want a dress that flashes like the stars."

When she appeared at the ball the bride was in ecstasies over the new dress, and said, "I must and will have it," and the owner consented to give it to her on the same condition.

This time the bridegroom did not drink the wine on retiring to rest, but poured it under the bed.

When all the house was still he heard a soft voice saying:

> " Drummer, drummer, listen to me.
> Have you forgotten me quite?"

Suddenly his memory returned. "Ah," he cried, "how faithless and cruel I have been! But the kiss which in the joy of my heart I pressed on my parents' right cheek is really to blame." He jumped up, took the Princess by the hand, and led her to his parents' bedside. "Here is my true bride," he said; "if I marry the other I shall do her a great wrong."

The wedding festivities began over again, and the first bride was allowed to keep the three lovely dresses as compensation, and expressed herself satisfied.

ROSEBUD

NCE upon a time there lived a King and Queen who had no children; and this they lamented very much. But one day as the Queen was walking by the side of the river, a little fish lifted its head out of the water, and said, "Your wish shall be fulfilled, and you shall soon have a daughter." What the little fish had foretold soon came to pass; and the Queen had a little girl that was so very beautiful that the King could not cease looking on her for joy, and determined to hold a great feast. So he invited not only his relations, friends, and neighbours, but also all the fairies, that they might be kind and good to his little daughter. Now there were thirteen fairies in his kingdom, and he had only twelve golden dishes for them to eat out of, so that he was obliged to leave one of the fairies without an invitation. The rest came, and after the feast was over they gave all their best gifts to the little Princess: one gave her virtue, another beauty, another riches, and so on till she had all that was excellent in the world. When eleven had done blessing her, the thirteenth, who had not been invited, and was very angry on that account, came in, and determined to take her revenge. So she cried out, "The King's daughter shall in her fifteenth year be wounded by a spindle, and fall down dead." Then the twelfth, who had not yet given her gift, came forward and said, that the bad wish must be fulfilled, but that she could soften it, and that the King's daughter should not die, but fall asleep for a hundred years.

But the King hoped to save his dear child from the threatened evil, and ordered that all the spindles in the kingdom should be bought up and destroyed. All the fairies' gifts were in the meantime fulfilled; for the Princess was so beautiful, and well-behaved, and amiable, and wise, that every one who knew her loved her. Now it happened that on the very day she was fifteen years old the King and Queen were not at home, and she was left alone in the palace. So she roved about by herself, and looked at all the rooms and chambers, till at last she came to an old tower, to which there was a narrow staircase ending with a little door. In the door there was a golden key, and when she turned it the door sprang open, and there sat an old lady spinning away very busily. "Why, how now, good mother," said the Princess, "what are you doing there?" "Spinning," said the old lady, and nodded her head. "How prettily that little thing turns round!" said the Princess, and took the spindle and began to spin. But scarcely had she touched it, before the prophecy was fulfilled, and she fell down lifeless on the ground.

However, she was not dead, but had only fallen into a deep sleep; and the King and the Queen, who just then came home, and all their court, fell asleep too; and the horses slept in the stables, and the dogs in the court, the pigeons on the house-top and the flies on the walls. Even the fire on the hearth left off blazing, and went to sleep; and the meat that was roasting stood still; and the cook, who was at that moment pulling the kitchen-boy by the hair to give him a box on the ear for something he had done amiss, let him go, and both fell asleep; and so everything stood still, and slept soundly.

A large hedge of thorns soon grew round the palace, and every year it became higher and thicker, till at last the whole palace was surrounded and hid, so that not even the roof or the chimneys could be seen. But there went a report through all the land of the beautiful sleeping Rosebud (for so was the King's daughter called); so that from time to time several kings' sons came, and tried to break through the thicket into the palace. This they could never do; for the thorns and bushes laid hold of them as it were with hands, and there they stuck fast and died miserably.

After many many years there came a king's son into that land, and an old man told him the story of the thicket of thorns, and how a beautiful palace stood behind it, in which was a wondrous Princess, called Rosebud, asleep with all her court. He told too, how he had heard from his grandfather that many many princes had come, and had tried to break through the thicket, but had stuck fast and died. Then the young Prince said, "All this shall not frighten me, I will go and see Rosebud." The old man tried to dissuade him, but he persisted in going.

Now that very day were the hundred years completed; and as the Prince came to the thicket, he saw nothing but beautiful flowering shrubs, through which he passed with ease, and they closed after him as firm as ever. Then he came at last to the palace, and there in the court lay the dogs asleep, and the horses in the stables, and on the roof sat the pigeons fast asleep with their heads under their wings; and when he came into the palace, the flies slept on the walls, and the cook in the kitchen was still holding up her hand as if she would beat the boy, and the maid sat with a black fowl in her hand ready to be plucked.

Then he went on still further, and all was so still that he could hear every breath he drew; till at last he came to the old tower and opened the door of the little room in which Rosebud was, and there she lay fast asleep, and looked so beautiful that he could not take his eyes off her, and he stooped down and gave her a kiss. But the moment he kissed her she opened her eyes and awoke, and smiled upon him. Then they went out together, and presently the King and Queen also awoke, and all the court, and they gazed on each other with great wonder. And the horses got up and shook themselves, and the dogs jumped about and barked; the pigeons took their heads from under their wings, and looked about and flew into the fields; the flies on the walls buzzed away; the fire in the kitchen blazed up and cooked the dinner, and the roast meat turned round again; the cook gave the boy the box on his ear so that he cried out, and the maid went on plucking the fowl. And then was the wedding of the Prince and Rosebud celebrated, and they lived happily together all their lives long.

THE SPINDLE, THE SHUTTLE, AND THE NEEDLE

YOUNG girl had lost her parents when she was very young. She had a godmother, who lived all alone in a little cottage at the end of the village, and lived on what she earned by her needle, her spindle, and her shuttle. This good woman had taken the orphan home, and had taught her to work, and brought her up in piety and the fear of God.

When the young girl was fifteen years old her godmother fell sick. She called the child to her bedside and said, "Dear child, I feel that my end is near. I leave you my cottage; it will protect you against wind and rain. I also give you my spindle, my shuttle, and my needle, which will enable you to earn your living."

Then placing her hand upon the girl's head she blessed her, and said, "Keep your heart pure and honest, and happiness will come to you." Then her eyes closed; the poor girl went weeping beside her godmother's coffin to the graveside.

After this she lived all alone, working bravely at weaving, spinning, and sewing; and the blessing of the good old woman kept her from harm. One would have thought that her stock of flax would never run out, and as soon as she had woven a piece of stuff, or made a shirt, a purchaser was sure to come and pay well for it; so that not only was she free from want, but had even something to give to the poor.

About this time the King's son came roaming through the country in search of a wife. He could not choose a poor one, and he did not like a rich one. So he said he would choose the girl who was at the same time the poorest and the richest. On coming to the village where our young girl lived, he asked, according to his wont, to be shown the poorest and the richest girl in the place. The richest was quickly found; as for the poorest, they told him it must be the young girl who lived in the lonely cottage at the end of the hamlet.

When the Prince passed by the rich girl was sitting dressed in her best in front of her door; she rose and went towards him with a profound curtsy. But he looked at her, and without a word passed on. He then came to the cottage of the poor girl; she was not at the door, but shut up in her room. He stopped and looked through the window into the room, which a ray of the sun lighted up. She was sitting at her spinning-wheel, working industriously. On her part she secretly observed the Prince looking at her; but she blushed scarlet, and continued spinning with her eyes cast down; only I won't warrant

K·N

that her thread was quite even. She went on spinning until the Prince was gone. So soon as she had lost sight of him, she ran to open the window, saying, "It 's so hot here!" and she followed him with her eyes as long as she could perceive the plume on his hat.

At last she sat down again and resumed her spinning. But a rhyme she had often heard her old godmother sing came into her mind, and she sang :

> " Run without stopping, spindle dear ;
> See that thou bring my true love here ! "

And what happened? The spindle sprang suddenly from her hands and rushed out at the door. She followed it with her eyes, quite stupefied with wonder. It ran and danced across the fields, leaving a thread of gold behind it. In a little while it had gone too far for her to see. Having no spindle, she took her shuttle, and began to weave.

The spindle ran on and on, and by the time its thread was all unwound it had overtaken the Prince. "What do I see?" he cried. "This spindle wants to conduct me somewhere." Turning his horse, he galloped back, guided by the golden thread. The young girl continued working, singing the while:

> " Run out to meet him, shuttle dear ;
> See thou guide my bridegroom here."

Then the shuttle sprang from her hands and hopped out at the door. But, arrived on the threshold, it began to weave the most splendid carpet ever seen. On each side were garlands of roses and lilies, and in the centre green vines grew out of a golden ground. Hares and rabbits were represented jumping in the leaves, and stags and squirrels looked out from among them. On the branches were perched birds of a thousand hues, who only wanted voice to make them perfect. The shuttle went on running, and the carpet-weaving advanced marvellously.

As she had lost her shuttle, the young girl took her needle, and began singing :

" He 's coming, he 's coming, my needle dear ;
See thou that all things are ready here."

The needle jumped from her fingers and began running round the room as quick as lightning. It was as if little invisible spirits had taken up the matter; the tables and benches covered themselves with green tapestry, the chairs were dressed in velvet, and silken hangings appeared on the walls.

Scarcely had the needle pierced its last stitch when the girl saw the white plume of the Prince's hat pass the window. He had been brought back by the golden thread. He entered the room, stepping over the carpet, and there he saw the young girl still dressed in her poor clothes, but shining among all this sudden splendour like a wild rose on a bush.

" Thou art at once the poorest and the richest," he cried. " Come, thou shalt be my wife."

She held out her hand to him without replying. He gave her a kiss, lifted her on his horse, and carried her off to the court, where their wedding was celebrated with great rejoicings.

As for the spindle, the shuttle, and the needle, they were carefully preserved in the royal treasury.

SNOWDROP

T was in the middle of winter, when the broad flakes of snow were falling around, that a certain Queen sat working at a window, the frame of which was made of fine black ebony; and as she was looking out upon the snow, she pricked her finger, and three drops of blood fell upon it. Then she gazed thoughtfully upon the red drops which sprinkled the white snow, and said, "Would that my little daughter may be as white as that snow, as red as the blood, and as black as the ebony window-frame!" And so the little girl grew up: her skin was as white as snow, her cheeks as rosy as the blood, and her hair as black as ebony; and she was called Snowdrop.

But this Queen died; and the King soon married another wife, who was very beautiful, but so proud that she could not bear to think that any one could surpass her. She had a magical looking-glass, to which she used to go and gaze upon herself in it, and say:

"Tell me, glass, tell me true!
Of all the ladies in the land,
Who is the fairest? tell me who?"

And the glass answered:

> "Thou, Queen, art fairest in the land."

But Snowdrop grew more and more beautiful; and when she was seven years old she was as bright as the day, and fairer than the Queen herself. Then the glass one day answered the Queen, when she went to consult it as usual:

> "Thou, Queen, may'st fair and beauteous be,
> But Snowdrop is lovelier far than thee!"

When she heard this, she turned pale with rage and envy; and called to one of her servants and said, "Take Snowdrop away into the wide wood, that I may never see her more." Then the servant led her away; but his heart melted when she begged him to spare her life, and he said, "I will not hurt thee, thou pretty child." So he left her by herself; and though he thought it most likely that the wild beasts would tear her in pieces, he felt as if a great weight were taken off his heart when he had made up his mind not to kill her, but leave her to her fate.

Then poor Snowdrop wandered along through the wood in great fear; and the wild beasts roared about her, but none did her any harm. In the evening she came to a little cottage, and went in there to rest herself, for her little feet would carry her no further. Everything was spruce and neat in the cottage: on the table was spread a white cloth, and there were seven little plates with seven little loaves, and seven little glasses with wine in them; and knives and forks laid in order; and by the wall stood seven little beds. Then, as she was very hungry, she picked a little piece off each loaf, and drank a very little wine out of each glass; and after that she thought she would lie down and rest. So she tried all the little beds; and one was too long, and another was too short, till at last the seventh suited her; and there she laid herself down, and went to sleep.

Presently in came the masters of the cottage, who were seven little dwarfs that lived among the mountains, and dug and searched about for gold. They lighted up their seven lamps, and saw directly that all was not right. The first said, "Who has been sitting on my stool?" The second, "Who has been eating off my plate?" The third, "Who has been picking my bread?" The fourth, "Who has been meddling with my spoon?" The fifth, "Who has been handling my fork?" The sixth, "Who has been cutting with my knife?" The seventh, "Who has been drinking my wine?" Then the first looked round and said, "Who has been lying on my bed?" And the rest came running to him, and every one cried out that somebody had been upon his bed. But the seventh saw Snowdrop, and called all his brethren to come and see her; and they cried out with wonder and astonishment, and brought their lamps to look at her, and said, "Good heavens! what a lovely child she is!" And they were delighted to see her, and took care not to wake her; and the seventh dwarf slept an hour with each of the other dwarfs in turn, till the night was gone.

In the morning Snowdrop told them all her story; and they pitied her, and said if she would keep all things in order, and cook and wash, and knit and spin for them, she might stay where she was, and they would take good care of her. Then they went out all day long to their work, seeking for gold and silver in the mountains; and Snowdrop remained at home: and they warned her, and said, "The Queen will soon find out where you are, so take care and let no one in."

But the Queen, now that she thought Snowdrop was dead, believed that she was certainly the handsomest lady in the land; and she went to her glass and said:

"Tell me, glass, tell me true!
Of all the ladies in the land,
Who is the fairest? tell me who?"

And the glass answered:

"Thou, Queen, art the fairest in all this land;
But over the hills, in the greenwood shade,
Where the seven dwarfs their dwelling have made,
There Snowdrop is hiding her head, and she
Is lovelier far, O Queen! than thee."

Then the Queen was very much alarmed; for she knew that the glass always spoke the truth, and was sure that the servant had betrayed her. And she could not bear to think that any one lived who was more beautiful than she was; so she disguised herself as an old pedlar, and went her way over the hills to the place where the dwarfs dwelt. Then she knocked at the door, and cried, " Fine wares to sell! " Snowdrop looked out at the window, and said, " Good-day, good woman; what have you to sell? " " Good wares, fine wares," said she; " laces and bobbins of all colours." " I will let the old lady in; she seems to be a very good sort of body," thought Snowdrop; so she ran down, and unbolted the door. " Bless me! " said the old woman, " how badly your stays are laced! Let me lace them up with one of my nice new laces." Snowdrop did not dream of any mischief; so she stood up before the old woman; but she set to work so nimbly, and pulled the lace so tight, that Snowdrop lost her breath, and fell down as if she were dead. "There's an end of all thy beauty," said the spiteful Queen, and went away home.

In the evening the seven dwarfs returned; and I need not say how grieved they were to see their faithful Snowdrop stretched upon the ground motionless, as if she were quite dead. However, they lifted her up, and when they found what was the matter, they cut the lace; and in a little time she began to breathe, and soon came to life again. Then they said, " The old woman was the Queen herself; take care another time, and let no one in when we are away."

When the Queen got home, she went straight to her

glass, and spoke to it as usual; but to her great surprise it still said:

> " Thou, Queen, art the fairest in all this land ;
> But over the hills, in the greenwood shade,
> Where the seven dwarfs their dwelling have made,
> There Snowdrop is hiding her head, and she
> Is lovelier far, O Queen ! than thee."

Then the blood ran cold in her heart with spite and malice to see that Snowdrop still lived; and she dressed herself up again in a disguise, but very different from the one she wore before, and took with her a poisoned comb. When she reached the dwarfs' cottage, she knocked at the door, and cried, " Fine wares to sell!" But Snowdrop said, " I dare not let any one in." Then the Queen said, " Only look at my beautiful combs"; and gave her the poisoned one. And it looked so pretty that she took it up and put it into her hair to try it; but the moment it touched her head the poison was so powerful that she fell down senseless. " There you may lie," said the Queen, and went her way. But by good luck the dwarfs returned very early that evening; and when they saw Snowdrop lying on the ground, they thought what had happened, and soon found the poisoned comb. And when they took it away, she recovered, and told them all that had passed; and they warned her once more not to open the door to any one.

Meantime the Queen went home to her glass, and trembled with rage when she received exactly the same answer as before; and she said, "Snowdrop shall die, if it costs me my life." So she went secretly into a chamber, and prepared a poisoned apple: the outside looked very rosy and tempting, but whoever tasted it was sure to die. Then she dressed herself up as a peasant's wife, and travelled over the hills to the dwarfs' cottage, and knocked at the door; but Snowdrop put her head out of the window and said, "I dare not let any one in, for the dwarfs have told me not to." "Do as you please," said the old woman, "but at any rate take this pretty apple; I will make you a present of it." "No," said Snowdrop, "I dare not take it." "You silly girl!" answered the other, "what are you afraid of? do you think it is poisoned? Come! do you eat one part, and I will eat the other." Now the apple was so prepared that one side was good, though the other side was poisoned. Then Snowdrop was very much tempted to taste, for the apple looked exceedingly nice; and when she saw the old woman eat, she could refrain no longer. But she had scarcely put the piece into her mouth, when she fell down dead upon the ground. "This time nothing will save thee," said the Queen; and she went home to her glass, and at last it said:

"Thou, Queen, art the fairest of all the fair."

And then her envious heart was glad, and as happy as such a heart could be.

When evening came, and the dwarfs returned home, they found Snowdrop lying on the ground: no breath passed her lips, and they were afraid that she was quite dead. They lifted her up, and combed her hair, and washed her face with wine and water; but all was in vain, for the little girl seemed quite dead. So they laid her down upon a bier, and all seven watched and bewailed her three whole days; and then they proposed to bury her: but her cheeks were still rosy, and her face looked just as it did while she was alive; so they said, "We will never bury her in the cold ground." And they made a coffin of glass, so that they might still look at her, and wrote her name upon it, in golden letters, and that she was a king's daughter. And the coffin was placed upon the hill, and one of the dwarfs always sat by it and watched. And the birds of the air came, too, and bemoaned Snowdrop: first of all came an owl, and then a raven, but at last came a dove.

And thus Snowdrop lay for a long long time, and still only looked as though she were asleep; for she was even now as white as snow, and as red as blood, and as black as ebony. At last a Prince came and called at the dwarfs' house; and he saw Snowdrop, and read what was written in golden letters. Then he offered the dwarfs money, and earnestly prayed them to let him take her away; but they said, "We will not part with her for all the gold in the world." At last, however, they had pity on him, and gave him the coffin: but the moment he lifted it up to carry it home with him, the piece of apple fell from between her lips, and Snowdrop awoke, and said, "Where am I?" And the Prince answered, "Thou art safe with me." Then he told her all that had happened, and said, "I love you better than all the world: come with me to my father's palace, and you shall be my wife." And Snowdrop consented, and went home with the Prince; and everything was prepared with great pomp and splendour for their wedding.

To the feast was invited, among the rest, Snowdrop's old enemy the Queen; and as she was dressing herself in fine rich clothes, she looked in the glass, and said:

> " Tell me, glass, tell me true !
> Of all the ladies in the land,
> Who is the fairest ? tell me who ? "

And the glass answered:

> " Thou, lady, art loveliest *here*, I ween ;
> But lovelier far is the new-made Queen."

When she heard this she started with rage; but her envy and curiosity were so great, that she could not help setting out to see the bride. And when she arrived and saw that it was no other than Snowdrop, who, as she thought, had been dead a long while, she choked with passion, and fell ill and died; but Snowdrop and the Prince lived and reigned happily over that land many many years.

JORINDE AND JORINGEL

NCE upon a time, in a castle in the midst of a large thick wood, there lived an old witch all by herself. By day she changed herself into a cat or an owl; but in the evening she resumed her right form. She was ablc also to allure to her the wild animals and birds, whom she killed, cooked, and ate, for whoever ventured within a hundred steps of her castle was obliged to stand still, and could not stir from the spot until she allowed it; but if a pretty maiden came into the circle the witch changed her into a bird, and then put her into a basket, which she carried into one of the rooms in the castle; and in this room were already many thousand such baskets of rare birds.

Now there was a young maiden called Jorinde, who was exceedingly pretty, and she was betrothed to a youth named Joringel, and just at the time that the events which I am about to relate happened, they were passing the days together in a round of pleasure. One day they went into the forest for a walk, and Joringel said, " Take care that you do not go too near the castle." It was a beautiful evening, the sun shining between the stems of the trees, and brightening up the dark green leaves, and the turtle-doves cooing softly upon the may-bushes. Jorinde began to cry, and sat down in the sunshine with Joringel, who cried too, for they were quite frightened, and thought they should die, when they looked round and saw how far they had wandered, and that there was no house in sight. The sun was yet half above the hills and half below, and Joringel, looking through the brushwood, saw the old walls of the castle close by them, which frightened him terribly, so that he fell off his seat. Then Jorinde sang:

"My little bird, with his ring so red,
  Sings sorrow, and sorrow and woe;
For he sings that the turtle-dove soon will be dead,
  Oh, sorrow, and sorrow—jug, jug, jug."

Joringel lifted up his head, and saw Jorinde was changed into a nightingale, which was singing, "Jug, jug, jug," and presently an owl flew round thrice, with his eyes glistening, and crying, "Tu wit, tu woo." Joringel could not stir; there he stood like a stone, and could not weep, nor speak, nor move hand or foot. Meanwhile the sun set, and, the owl flying into a bush, out came an ugly old woman, thin and yellow, with great red eyes, and a crooked nose which reached down to her chin. She muttered and seized the nightingale, and carried it away in her hand, while Joringel remained

KN.

there incapable of moving or speaking. At last the witch returned, and said, with a hollow voice, "Greet you, Zachiel! if the moon shines on your side, release this one at once." Then Joringel became free, and fell down on his knees before the witch, and begged her to give him back Jorinde; but she refused, and said he should never again have her, and went away. He cried, and wept, and groaned after her, but all to no purpose; at length he rose and went into a strange village, where for some time he tended sheep. He often went round about the enchanted castle, but never too near, and one night after so walking, he dreamt that he found a blood-red flower, in the middle of which lay a fine pearl. This flower, he thought, he broke off, and, going therewith to the castle, all he touched with it was free from enchantment, and thus he regained his Jorinde.

When he awoke next morning he began his search over hill and valley to find such a flower, but nine days had passed away. At length, early one morning, he discovered it, and in its middle was a large dewdrop, like a beautiful pearl. Then he carried the flower day and night, till he came to the castle; and, although he ventured within the enchanted circle, he was not stopped, but walked on quite to the door. Joringel was now in high spirits, and touching the door with his flower it flew open. He entered, and passed through the hall, listening for the sound of the birds, which at last he heard. He found the room, and went in, and there was the enchantress feeding the birds in the seven thousand baskets. As soon as she saw Joringel she became frightfully enraged, and spat out poison and gall at him, but she dared not come too close. He would not turn back for her, but looked at the baskets of birds; but, alas! there were many hundreds of nightingales, and how was he to know his Jorinde? While he was examining them he perceived the old woman secretly taking away one of the baskets, and slipping out of the door. Joringel flew after her, and touched the basket with his flower, and also the old woman, so that she could no longer bewitch; and at once Jorinde stood before him, and fell upon his neck, as beautiful as she ever was. Afterwards he disenchanted all the other birds, and then returned home with his Jorinde, and for many years they lived together happily and contentedly.

THE GOOSE GIRL

N old Queen, whose husband had been dead some years, had a beautiful daughter. When she grew up, she was betrothed to a Prince who lived a great way off; and as the time drew near for her to be married, shc got rcady to sct off on hcr journey to his country. Then the Queen her mother packed up a great many costly things; jewels, and gold, and silver; trinkets, fine dresses, and in short everything that became a royal bride; for she loved her child very dearly: and she gave her a waiting-maid to ride with her, and give her into the bridegroom's hands; and each had a horse for the journey. Now the Princess's horse was called Falada, and could speak.

When the time came for them to set out, the old Queen went into her bedchamber, and took a little knife, and cut off a lock of her hair, and gave it to her daughter, and said, "Take care of it, dear child; for it is a charm that may be of use to you on the road." Then they took a sorrowful leave of each other, and the Princess put the lock of her mother's hair into her bosom, got upon her horse, and set off on her journey to her bridegroom's kingdom. One day, as they were riding along by the side of a brook, the Princess began to feel very thirsty, and said to her maid, "Pray get down and fetch me some water in my golden cup out of yonder brook, for I want to drink." "Nay," said the maid, "if you are thirsty, get down yourself, and lie down by the water and drink; I shall not be your waiting-maid any longer." Then she was so thirsty that she got down, and knelt over the little brook, and drank, for she was frightened, and dared not bring out her golden cup; and then she wept, and said, "Alas! what will become of me?" And the lock of hair answered her, and said:

> "Alas! alas! if thy mother knew it,
> Sadly, sadly her heart would rue it."

But the Princess was very humble and meek, so she said nothing to her maid's ill behaviour, but got upon her horse again.

Then all rode further on their journey, till the day grew so warm, and the sun so scorching, that the bride began to feel very thirsty again; and at last when they came to a river she forgot her maid's rude speech, and said, "Pray get down and fetch me some water to drink in my golden cup." But the maid answered her, and even spoke more haughtily than before, "Drink if you will, but I shall not be your waiting-maid." Then the Princess was so thirsty that she got off her horse, and lay down, and held her head over the running stream, and cried, and said, "What will become of me?" And the lock of hair answered her again:

> "Alas! alas! if thy mother knew it,
> Sadly, sadly her heart would rue it."

And as she leaned down to drink, the lock of hair fell from her bosom, and floated away with the water, without her seeing it, she was so frightened. But her maid saw it, and was very glad, for she knew the charm, and saw that the poor bride would be in her power, now that she had lost the hair. So when the bride had done, and would have got upon Falada again, the maid said, "I shall ride upon Falada, and you may have my horse instead": so she was forced to give up her horse, and soon afterwards to take off her royal clothes, and put on her maid's shabby ones.

At last, as they drew near the end of their journey, this treacherous servant threatened to kill her mistress if she ever told any one what had happened. But Falada saw it all, and marked it well. Then the waiting-maid got upon Falada, and the real bride was set upon the other horse, and they went on in this way till at last they came to the royal court. There was great joy at their coming, and the Prince flew to meet them, and lifted the maid from her horse, thinking she was the one who was to be his wife; and she was led up stairs to the royal chamber, but the true Princess was told to stay in the court below.

But the old King happened to be looking out of the window, and saw her in the yard below; and as she looked very pretty, and too delicate for a waiting-maid, he went into the royal chamber to ask the bride who it was she had brought with her, that was thus left standing in the court below. "I brought her with me for the sake of her company on the road," said she; "pray give the girl some work to do, that she may not be idle." The old King could not for some time think of any work for her to do; but at last he said, "I have a lad who takes care of my geese; she may go and help him." Now the name of this lad, that the real bride was to help in watching the King's geese, was Curdken.

Soon after, the false bride said to the Prince, "Dear husband, pray do me one piece of kindness." "That I will," said the Prince. "Then tell one of your slaughterers to cut off the head of the horse I rode upon, for it was very unruly, and plagued me sadly on the road": but the truth was, she was very much afraid lest Falada should speak, and tell all she had done to the Princess. She carried her point, and the faithful Falada was killed: but when the true Princess heard of it, she wept, and begged the man to nail up Falada's head against a large dark gate of the city, through which she had to pass every morning and evening, that there she might still see him sometimes. Then the slaughterer said he would do as she wished; and cut off the head, and nailed it fast under the dark gate.

Early the next morning, as she and Curdken went out through the gate, she said sorrowfully:

" Falada, Falada, there thou art hanging ! "

and the head answered:

" Bride, bride, there thou art ganging !
Alas ! alas ! if thy mother knew it,
Sadly, sadly her heart would rue it."

Then they went out of the city, and drove the geese on. And when she came to the meadow, she sat down upon a bank there, and let down her waving locks of hair, which were all of pure silver; and when Curdken saw it glitter in the sun, he ran up, and would have pulled some of the locks out; but she cried:

" Blow, breezes, blow !
Let Curdken's hat go !
Blow, breezes, blow !
Let him after it go !
O'er hills, dales, and rocks,
Away be it whirl'd,
Till the silvery locks
Are all comb'd and curl'd ! "

Then there came a wind, so strong that it blew off Curdken's hat; and away it flew over the hills, and he after it; till, by the time he came back, she had done combing and curling her hair, and put it up again safe. Then he was very angry and sulky, and would not speak to her at all; but they watched the geese until it grew dark in the evening, and then drove them homewards.

The next morning, as they were going through the dark gate, the poor girl looked up at Falada's head, and cried:

> "Falada, Falada, there thou art hanging!"

and it answered:

> "Bride, bride, there thou art ganging!
> Alas! alas! if thy mother knew it,
> Sadly, sadly her heart would rue it."

Then she drove on the geese, and sat down again in the meadow, and began to comb out her hair as before; and Curdken ran up to her, and wanted to take hold of it; but she cried out quickly:

> "Blow, breezes, blow!
> Let Curdken's hat go!
> Blow, breezes, blow!
> Let him after it go!
> O'er hills, dales, and rocks,
> Away be it whirl'd,
> Till the silvery locks
> Are all comb'd and curl'd!"

Then the wind came and blew his hat, and off it flew a great way, over the hills and far away, so that he had to run after it; and when he came back, she had done up her hair again, and all was safe. So they watched the geese till it grew dark.

In the evening, after they came home, Curdken went to the old King, and said, "I cannot have that strange girl to help me to keep the geese any longer." "Why?"

said the King. " Because she does nothing but tease me all day long." Then the King made him tell him all that had passed. And Curdken said, " When we go in the morning through the dark gate with our flock of geese, she weeps, and talks with the head of a horse that hangs upon the wall, and says:

> ' Falada, Falada, there thou art hanging ! '

and the head answers:

> ' Bride, bride, there thou art ganging !
> Alas ! alas ! if thy mother knew it,
> Sadly, sadly her heart would rue it.' "

And Curdken went on telling the King what had happened upon the meadow where the geese fed; and how his hat was blown away, and he was forced to run after it, and leave his flock. But the old King told him to go out again as usual the next day: and when morning came, he placed himself behind the dark gate, and heard how she spoke to Falada, and how Falada answered ; and then he went into the field, and hid himself in a bush by the meadow's side, and soon saw with his own eyes how they drove the flock of geese, and how, after a little time, she let down her hair that glittered in the sun; and then he heard her say :

> " Blow, breezes, blow !
> Let Curdken's hat go !
> Blow, breezes, blow !
> Let him after it go !

O'er hills, dales, and rocks,
Away be it whirl'd,
Till the silvery locks
Are all comb'd and curl'd!"

And soon came a gale of wind, and carried away Curdken's hat, while the girl went on combing and curling her hair. All this the old King saw: so he went home without being seen; and when the little goose girl came back in the evening, he called her aside, and asked her why she did so: but she burst into tears, and said, "That I must not tell you or any man, or I shall lose my life."

But the old King begged so hard, that she had no peace till she had told him all, word for word: and it was very lucky for her that she did so, for the King ordered royal clothes to be put upon her, and gazed on her with wonder, she was so beautiful. Then he called his son, and told him, that he had only the false bride, for that she was merely a waiting-maid, while the true one stood by. And the young King rejoiced when he saw her beauty, and heard how meek and patient she had been; and, without saying anything, ordered a great feast to be got ready for all his court. The bridegroom sat at the top, with the false Princess on one side, and the true one on the other; but nobody knew her, for she was quite dazzling to their eyes, and was not at all like the little goose girl, now that she had her brilliant dress.

When they had eaten and drunk, and were very merry,

the old King told all the story, as one that he had once heard of, and asked the true waiting-maid what she thought ought to be done to any one who would behave thus. "Nothing better," said this false bride, "than that she should be thrown into a cask stuck round with sharp nails, and that two white horses should be put to it, and should drag it from street to street till she is dead." "Thou art she!" said the old King, "and since thou hast judged thyself, it shall be so done to thee." And the young King was married to his true wife, and they reigned over the kingdom in peace and happiness all their lives.

CLEVER ALICE

NCE upon a time there was a man who had a daughter, who was called "Clever Alice"; and when she was grown up, her father said, "We must see about her marrying." "Yes," replied her mother, "when one comes who shall be worthy of her." At last a certain youth, by name Hans, came from a distance to make a proposal for her, but he put in one condition, that Clever Alice should also be very prudent. "Oh," said her father, "she has got a head full of brains"; and the mother added, "Ah, she can hear the wind blow up the street, and hear the flies cough!"

"Very well," replied Hans, "but if she is not very prudent, I will not have her." Soon afterwards they sat down to dinner, and her mother said, "Alice, go down into the cellar and draw some beer."

So Clever Alice took the jug down from the wall and went into the cellar, jerking the lid up and down on her way to pass away the time. As soon as she got downstairs she drew a stool and placed it before the cask, in order that she might not have to stoop, whereby she might do some injury to her back, and give it an undesirable bend. Then she placed the can before her and turned the tap, and while the beer was running, as she did not wish her eyes to be idle, she looked about upon the wall above and below, and presently perceived, after much peeping into this and that corner, a hatchet, which the bricklayers had left behind, sticking out of the ceiling right above her. At the sight of this the Clever Alice began to cry, saying, "Oh, if I marry Hans, and we have a child, and he grow up, and we send him into the cellar to draw beer, the hatchet will fall upon his head and kill him!" and so saying, she sat there weeping with all her might over the impending misfortune.

Meanwhile the good folks upstairs were waiting for the beer, but as Clever Alice did not come, her mother told the maid to go and see what she was stopping for. The maid went down into the cellar and found Alice sitting before the cask crying heartily, and she asked, "Alice, what are you weeping about?" "Ah," she replied, "have I not cause? If I marry Hans, and we have a child, and he grow up, and we send him here to draw beer, that hatchet will fall upon his head and kill him."

"Oh," said the maid, "what a Clever Alice we have!" And, sitting down, she began to weep, too, for the misfortune that was to happen.

After a while, and the maid did not return, the good folks above began to feel very thirsty; so the husband told the boy to go down into the cellar, and see what had become of Alice and the maid. The boy went down, and there sat Clever Alice and the maid both crying, so he asked the reason; and Alice told him the same tale of the hatchet that was to fall on her child, as she had told the maid. When she had finished, the boy exclaimed, "What a Clever Alice we have!" and fell weeping and howling with the others.

Upstairs they were still waiting, and the husband said, when the boy did not return, "Do you go down, wife, into the cellar and see why Alice stops." So she went down, and finding all three sitting there crying, asked the reason, and Alice told her about the hatchet which must inevitably fall upon the head of her son. Then the mother likewise exclaimed, "Oh, what a Clever Alice we have!" and, sitting down, began to weep with the others. Meanwhile the husband waited for his wife's return; but at last he felt so very thirsty that he said, "I must go myself down into the cellar and see what Alice stops for." As soon as he entered the cellar, there he found the four sitting and crying together, and when he heard the reason, he also exclaimed, "Oh, what a Clever Alice we have!" and sat down to cry with the others. All this time the bridegroom above sat waiting, but when nobody returned he thought they must be waiting for him, and so he went down to see what was the matter. When he entered, there sat the five crying and groaning, each one in a louder key than his neighbour. "What misfortune has happened?" he asked. "Ah, dear Hans!" cried Alice, "if we should marry one another, and have a child, and he grow up, and we, perhaps, send him down here to tap the beer, the hatchet which has been left sticking there may fall on his head, and so kill him; and do you not think that enough to weep about?"

"Now," said Hans, "more prudence than this is not necessary for my housekeeping; because you are such a Clever Alice I will have you for my wife." And, taking her hand, he led her home, and celebrated the wedding directly.

After they had been married a little while, Hans said one morning, "Wife, I will go out to work and earn some money; do you go into the field and gather some corn wherewith to make bread."

"Yes," she answered, "I will do so, dear Hans." And when he was gone, she cooked herself a nice mess of pottage to take with her. As she came to the field, she said to herself, "What shall I do? Shall I cut first, or eat first? Ay, I will eat first!" Then she ate up the contents of her pot, and when it was finished, she thought to herself, "Now, shall I reap first or sleep first? Well, I think I will have a nap!" and so she laid herself down amongst the corn, and went to sleep. Meanwhile Hans returned home, but Alice did not come, and so he said, "Oh, what a prudent Alice I have; she is so industrious that she does not even come

K
N

home to eat anything." By and by, however, evening came on, and still she did not return; so Hans went out to see how much she had reaped; but, behold, nothing at all, and there lay Alice fast asleep among the corn! So home he ran very fast, and brought a net with little bells hanging on it, which he threw over her head while she still slept on. When he had done this, he went back again and shut to the house door, and, seating himself on his stool, began working very industriously.

At last, when it was quite dark, Clever Alice awoke, and as soon as she stood up, the net fell all over her hair, and the bells jingled at every step she took. This quite frightened her, and she began to doubt whether she were really Clever Alice, and said to herself, "Am I she, or am I not?" This question she could not answer, and she stood still a long while considering. At last she thought she would go home and ask whether she were really herself—supposing they would be able to tell. When she came to the house door it was shut; so she tapped at the window, and asked, "Hans, is Alice within?" "Yes," he replied, "she is." Now she was really terrified, and exclaiming, "Ah, heaven, then I am not Alice!" she ran up to another house; but as soon as the folks within heard the jingling of the bells they would not open their doors, and so nobody would receive her. Then she ran straight away from the village, and no one has ever seen her since.

CHERRY, OR THE FROG BRIDE

HERE was once a King who had three sons. Not far from his kingdom lived an old woman who had an only daughter called Cherry. The King sent his sons out to see the world, that they might learn the ways of foreign lands, and get wisdom and skill in ruling the kingdom that they were one day to have for their own. But the old woman lived at peace at home with her daughter, who was called Cherry, because she liked cherries better than any other kind of food, and would eat scarcely anything else. Now her poor old mother had no garden, and no money to buy cherries every day for her daughter; and at last there was no other plan left but to go to a neighbouring nunnery-garden and beg the finest she could get of the nuns; for she dared not let her daughter go out by herself, as she was very pretty, and she feared some mischance might befall her. Cherry's taste was, however, very well known; and as it happened that the Abbess was as fond of cherries as she was, it was soon found out where all the best fruit went; and the Holy Mother was not a little angry at missing some of her stock and finding whither it had gone.

The Princes while wandering on came one day to the town where Cherry and her mother lived; and as they passed along the street they saw the fair maiden standing at the window, combing her long and beautiful locks of hair. Then each of the three fell deeply in love with her, and began to say how much he longed to have her for his wife! Scarcely had the wish been spoken, when all drew their swords, and a dreadful battle began; the fight lasted long, and their rage grew hotter and hotter, when at last the Abbess hearing the uproar came to the gate. Finding that her neighbour was the cause, her old spite against her broke forth at once, and in her rage she wished Cherry turned into an ugly frog, and sitting in the water under the bridge at the world's end. No sooner said than done; and poor Cherry became a frog, and vanished out of their sight. The Princes had now nothing to fight for; so sheathing their swords again, they shook hand as brothers, and went on towards their father's home.

The old King meanwhile found that he grew weak and ill-fitted for the business of reigning: so he thought of giving up his kingdom; but to whom should it be? This was a point that his fatherly heart could not settle; for he loved all his sons alike. "My dear children," said he, "I grow old and weak, and should like to give up my kingdom; but I cannot make up my mind which of you to choose for my heir, for I love you all three; and besides, I should wish to give my people the cleverest and best of you for their King. However, I will give you three trials, and the one who wins the prize shall have the kingdom. The first is to seek me out one hundred ells of cloth, so fine that I can draw it through my golden ring." The sons said they would do their best, and set out on the search.

The two eldest brothers took with them many followers, and coaches and horses of all sorts, to bring home all the beautiful cloths which they should find; but the youngest went alone by himself. They soon came to where the roads branched off into several ways; two ran through smiling meadows, with smooth paths and shady groves, but the third looked dreary and dirty, and went over barren wastes. The two eldest chose the pleasant ways; and the youngest took his leave and whistled along over the dreary road. Whenever fine linen was to be seen, the two elder brothers bought it, and bought so much that their coaches and horses bent under their burden. The youngest, on the other hand, journeyed on many a weary day, and found not a place where he could buy even one piece of cloth that was at all fine and good. His heart sank within him, and every mile he grew more and more heavy and sorrowful. At last he came to a bridge over a stream, and there he sat himself down to rest and sigh over his bad luck, when an ugly-looking frog popped its head out of the water, and asked, with a voice that had not at all a harsh sound to his ears, what was the matter. The Prince said in a pet, "Silly frog! thou canst not help me." "Who told you so?" said the frog; "tell me what ails you." After a while the Prince opened the whole story, and told why his father had sent him out. "I will help you," said the frog; so it jumped back into the stream and soon came back dragging a small piece of linen not bigger than one's hand, and by no means the cleanest in the world in its look. However, there it was, and the Prince was told to take it away with him. He had no great liking for such a dirty rag; but still there was something in the frog's speech that pleased him much, and he thought to himself, "It can do no harm, it is better than nothing"; so he picked it up, put it in his pocket, and thanked the frog, who dived down again, panting and quite tired, as it seemed, with its work. The further he went the heavier he found to his great joy the pocket grow, and so he turned himself homewards, trusting greatly in his good luck.

He reached home nearly about the same time that his brothers came up, with their horses and coaches all heavily laden. Then the old King was very glad to see his children again, and pulled the ring off his finger to try who had done the best; but in all the stock which the two eldest had brought there was not one piece a tenth part of which would go through the ring. At this they were greatly abashed; for they had made a laugh of their brother, who came home, as they thought, empty-handed. But how great was their anger when they saw him pull from his pocket a piece that for softness, beauty, and whiteness, was a thousand times better than anything that was ever before seen! It was so fine that it passed with ease through the ring; indeed, two such pieces would readily have gone in together. The father embraced the lucky youth, told his servants to throw the coarse linen into the sea, and said to his children, "Now you must set about the second task which I am to set you: bring me home a little dog, so small that it will lie in a nutshell."

His sons were not a little frightened at such a task; but they all longed for the crown, and made up their minds to go and try their hands, and so after a few days they set out once more on their travels. At the cross-ways they parted as before, and the youngest chose his old dreary rugged road with all the bright hopes that his former good luck gave him. Scarcely had he sat himself down again at the bridge foot, when his old friend the frog jumped out, set itself beside him, and as before opened its big wide mouth, and croaked out, "What is the matter?" The Prince had this time no doubt of the frog's power, and therefore told what he wanted. "It shall be done for you," said the frog; and springing into the stream it soon brought up a hazel-nut, laid it at his feet, and told him to take it home to his father, and crack it gently, and then see what would happen. The Prince went his way very well pleased, and the frog, tired with its task, jumped back into the water.

His brothers had reached home first, and brought with them a great many very pretty little dogs. The old King, willing to help them all he could, sent for a large walnut-shell and tried it with every one of the little dogs; but one stuck fast with the hind-foot out, and another with the head, and a third with the fore-foot, and a fourth with its tail—in short, some one way and some another; but none were at all likely to sit easily in this new kind of kennel. When all had been tried, the youngest made his father a dutiful bow, and gave him the hazel-nut, begging him to crack it very carefully: the moment this was done out ran a beautiful little white dog upon the King's hand, wagged its tail, fondled his new master, and soon turned about and barked at the other little beasts in the most graceful manner, to the delight of the whole court. The joy of every one was great; the old King again embraced his lucky son, told his people to drown all the other dogs in the sea, and said to his children, "Dear sons! your weightiest tasks are now over; listen to my last wish: whoever brings home the fairest lady shall be at once the heir to my crown."

The prize was so tempting and the chance so fair for all, that none made any doubts about setting to work, each in his own way, to try and be the winner. The

Rosebud looked so beautiful he stooped down
and gave her a kiss. (Page 72)

They wrote her name upon it, in golden
letters, and that she was a king's daughter. (Page 94)

youngest was not in such good spirits as he was the last time; he thought to himself, "The old frog has been able to do a great deal for me; but all its power must be nothing to me now, for where should it find me a fair maiden, still less a fairer maiden than was ever seen at my father's court? The swamps where it lives have no living things in them, but toads, snakes, and such vermin." Meantime he went on, and sighed as he sat down again with a heavy heart by the bridge. "Ah, Frog!" said he, "this time thou canst do me no good." "Never mind," croaked the frog; "only tell me what is the matter now." Then the Prince told his old friend what trouble had now come upon him. "Go thy ways home," said the frog; "the fair maiden will follow hard after; but take care and do not laugh at whatever may happen!" This said, it sprang as before into the water and was soon out of sight. The Prince still sighed on, for he trusted very little this time to the frog's word; but he had not set many steps towards home before he heard a noise behind him, and looking round saw six large water-rats dragging along a large pumpkin like a coach, full trot. On the box sat an old fat toad as coachman, and behind stood two little frogs as footmen, and two fine mice with stately whiskers ran before as outriders; within sat his old friend the frog, rather misshapen and unseemly to be sure, but still with somewhat of a graceful air as it bowed to him in passing. Much too deeply wrapt in thought as to his chance of finding the fair lady whom he was seeking to take any heed of the strange scene before him, the Prince scarcely looked at it, and had still less mind to laugh. The coach passed on a little way, and soon turned a corner that hid it from his sight; but how astonished was he, on turning the corner himself, to find a handsome coach and six black horses standing there, with a coachman in gay livery, and within, the most beautiful lady he had ever seen, whom he soon knew to be the fair Cherry, for whom his heart had so long ago panted! As he came up, the servants opened the coach door, and he was allowed to seat himself by the beautiful lady.

They soon came to his father's city, where his brothers also came, with trains of fair ladies; but as soon as Cherry was seen, all the court gave her with one voice the crown of beauty. The delighted father embraced his son, and named him the heir to his crown, and ordered all the other ladies to be thrown, like the little dogs, into the sea and drowned. Then the Prince married Cherry, and lived long and happily with her, and indeed lives with her still—if he be not dead.

THE THREE LITTLE MEN IN THE WOOD

NCE upon a time there lived a man, whose wife had died; and a woman, also, who had lost her husband: and this man and this woman had each a daughter. These two maidens were friendly with each other, and used to walk together, and one day they came by the widow's house. Then the widow said to the man's daughter, "Do you hear, tell your father I wish to marry him, and you shall every morning wash in milk and drink wine, but my daughter shall wash in water and drink water." So the girl went home and told her father what the woman had said, and he replied, "What shall I do? Marriage is a comfort, but it is also a torment." At last, as he could come to no conclusion, he drew off his boot, and said: "Take this boot, which has a hole in the sole, and go with it out of doors and hang it on the great nail, and then pour water into it. If it holds the water, I will again take a wife; but if it runs through, I will not have her." The girl did as he bid her, but the water drew the hole together and the boot became full to overflowing. So she told her father how it had happened, and he, getting up, saw it was quite true;

and going to the widow he settled the matter, and the wedding was celebrated.

The next morning, when the two girls arose, milk to wash in and wine to drink were set for the man's daughter, but only water, both for washing and drinking, for the woman's daughter. The second morning, water for washing and drinking stood before both the man's daughter and the woman's; and on the third morning, water to wash in and water to drink were set before the man's daughter, and milk to wash in and wine to drink before the woman's daughter, and so it continued.

Soon the woman conceived a deadly hatred for her stepdaughter, and knew not how to behave badly enough to her from day to day. She was envious, too, because her stepdaughter was beautiful and lovely, and her own daughter was ugly and hateful.

Once, in the winter time, when the river was frozen as hard as a stone, and hill and valley were covered with snow, the woman made a cloak of paper, and called the maiden to her and said, "Put on this cloak, and go away into the wood to fetch me a little basketful of strawberries, for I have a wish for some."

"Mercy on us!" said the maiden, "in winter there are no strawberries growing; the ground is frozen, and the snow, too, has covered everything. And why must I go in that paper cloak? It is so cold out of doors that it freezes one's breath even, and if the wind does not blow off this cloak the thorns will tear it from my body."

"Will you dare to contradict me?" said the step-mother. "Make haste off, and let me not see you again until you have found me a basket of strawberries." Then she gave her a small piece of dry bread, saying, "On that you must subsist the whole day." But she thought—out of doors she will be frozen and starved, so that my eyes will never see her again!

So the girl did as she was told, and put on the paper cloak, and went away with the basket. Far and near there was nothing but snow, and not a green blade was to be seen. When she came to the forest she discovered a little cottage, out of which three little dwarfs were peeping. The girl wished them good morning, and knocked gently at the door. They called her in, and entering the room, she sat down on a bench by the fire to warm herself and eat her breakfast. The dwarfs called out, "Give us some of it!" "Willingly," she replied, and, dividing her bread in two, she gave them half. They asked, "What do you here in the forest, in the winter time, in this thin cloak?"

"Ah!" she answered, "I must seek a basketful of strawberries, and I dare not return home until I can take them with me." When she had eaten her bread, they gave her a broom, saying, "Sweep away the snow with this from the back door." But when she was gone out of doors the three dwarfs said one to another, "What shall we give her, because she is so gentle and good, and has shared her bread with us?" Then said the first, "I grant to her that she shall become more beautiful every day." The second said, "I grant that a piece of gold shall fall out of her mouth for every word she speaks." The third said, "I grant that a king shall come and make her his bride."

Meanwhile, the girl had done as the dwarfs had bidden her, and had swept away the snow from behind the house. And what do you think she found there? Actually, ripe strawberries! which came quite red and sweet up under the snow. So filling her basket in great glee, she thanked the little men and gave them each her hand, and then ran home to take her stepmother what she wished for. As she went in and said, "Good evening," a piece of gold fell from her mouth. Thereupon she related what had happened to her in the forest; but at every word she spoke a piece of gold fell, so that the whole floor was covered.

"Just see her arrogance," said the stepsister, "to throw away money in that way!" but in her heart she was jealous, and wished to go into the forest too, to seek strawberries. Her mother said, "No, my dear daughter; it is too cold, you will be frozen!" but as her girl let her have no peace, she at last consented, and made her a beautiful fur cloak to put on; she also gave her buttered bread and cooked meat to eat on her way.

KN

The girl went into the forest and came straight to the little cottage. The three dwarfs were peeping out again, but she did not greet them; and, stumbling on without looking at them or speaking, she entered the room, and, seating herself by the fire, began to eat the bread and butter and meat. "Give us some of that," exclaimed the dwarfs; but she answered, "I have not got enough for myself, so how can I give any away?" When she had finished they said, "You have a broom there; go and sweep the back door clean." "Oh, sweep it yourself," she replied; "I am not your servant." When she saw that they would not give her anything she went out at the door, and the three dwarfs said to each other, "What shall we give her? she is so ill-behaved, and has such a bad and envious disposition, that nobody can wish well to her." The first said, "I grant that she becomes more ugly every day." The second said, "I grant that at every word she speaks a toad shall spring out of her mouth." The third said, "I grant that she shall die a miserable death." Meanwhile the girl had been looking for strawberries out of doors, but as she could find none she went home very peevish. When she opened her mouth to tell her mother what had happened to her in the forest, a toad jumped out of her mouth at each word, so that every one fled away from her in horror.

The step-mother was now still more vexed, and was always thinking how she could do the most harm to her husband's daughter, who every day became more beautiful. At last she took a kettle, set it on the fire, and boiled a net therein. When it was sodden she hung it on the shoulder of the poor girl, and gave her an axe, that she might go upon the frozen pond and cut a hole in the ice to drag the net. She obeyed, and went away and cut an ice hole; and while she was cutting, an elegant carriage came by, in which the King sat. The carriage stopped, and the King asked, "My child, who are you? and what do you here?" "I am a poor girl, and am dragging a net," said she. Then the King pitied her, and saw how beautiful she was, and said, "Will you go with me?" "Yes, indeed, with all my heart," she replied, for she was glad to get out of the sight of her mother and sister.

So she was handed into the carriage, and driven away with the King; and as soon as they arrived at his castle the wedding was celebrated with great splendour, as the dwarfs had granted to the maiden.

THE VALIANT LITTLE TAILOR

NE summer's morning a tailor was sitting on his bench by the window in very good spirits, sewing away with all his might, and presently up the street came a peasant woman, crying, "Good preserves for sale! Good preserves for sale!" This cry sounded nice in the tailor's ears, and, sticking his diminutive head out of the window, he called out, "Here, my good woman, just bring your wares here!" The woman mounted the three steps up to the tailor's house with her heavy basket, and began to unpack all the pots together before him. He looked at them all, held them up to the light, put his nose to them, and at last said, "These preserves appear to me to be very nice, so you may weigh me out four half-ounces, my good woman; I don't mind even if you make it a quarter of a pound." The woman, who expected to have met with a good customer, gave him what he wished, and went away grumbling, very much dissatisfied.

"Now!" exclaimed the tailor, "Heaven will send me a blessing on this preserve, and give me fresh strength and vigour"; and, taking the bread out of the cupboard, he cut himself a slice the size of the whole loaf, and spread the preserve upon it. "That will taste by no means badly," said he; "but, before I have a bite, I will just get this waistcoat finished." So he laid the bread down near him and stitched away, making larger and larger stitches every time for joy. Meanwhile the smell of the preserve mounted to the ceiling, where flies were sitting in great numbers, and enticed them down, so that soon a regular swarm of them had settled on the bread. "Holloa! who invited you?" exclaimed the tailor, hunting away the unbidden guests; but the flies, not understanding his language, would not be driven off, and came again in greater numbers than before. This put the little man in a boiling passion, and, snatching up in his rage a bag of cloth, he brought it down with an unmerciful swoop upon them. When he raised it again he counted no less than seven lying dead before him with outstretched legs. "What a fellow you are!" said he to himself, wondering at his own bravery. "The whole town shall know of this." In great haste he cut himself out a band, hemmed it, and then put on it in large characters, "SEVEN AT ONE BLOW!" "Ah," said he, "not one city alone, the whole world shall know it!" and his heart fluttered with joy, like a lambkin's tail.

The little tailor bound the belt round his body, and prepared to travel forth into the wide world, thinking

"Blow, breezes, blow!
Let Curdken's hat go!
Blow, breezes, blow!
Let him after it go!" (Page 111)

Within sat his old friend the frog. (Page 135)

the workshop too small for his valiant deeds. Before he set out, however, he looked round his house to see if there was anything he could take with him; but he found only an old cheese, which he pocketed, and remarking a bird before the door which was entangled in the bushes, he caught it, and put that in his pocket also. Directly after he set out bravely on his travels; and, as he was light and active, he felt no weariness. His road led him up a hill, and when he reached the highest point of it he found a great giant sitting there, who was looking about him very composedly.

The little tailor, however, went boldly up, and said, "Good day, comrade; in faith you sit there and see the whole world stretched below you. I am also on my road thither to try my luck. Have you a mind to go with me?"

The giant looked contemptuously at the little tailor, and said, "You vagabond; you miserable fellow!"

"That may be," replied the tailor; "but here you may read what sort of a man I am"; and, unbuttoning his coat, he showed the giant his belt. The giant read, "Seven at one blow"; and thinking they were men whom the tailor had slain, he conceived a little respect for him. Still he wished to prove him first; so taking up a stone, he squeezed it in his hand, so that water dropped out of it. "Do that after me," said he to the other, "if you have any strength."

"If it be nothing worse than that," said the tailor, "that 's play to me." And, diving into his pocket, he brought out the cheese, and squeezed it till the whey ran out of it, and said, "Now, I think, that 's a little better."

The giant did not know what to say, and could not believe it of the little man; so, taking up another stone, he threw it so high that one could scarcely see it with the eye, saying, "There, you manikin, do that after me."

"Well done," said the tailor; "but your stone must fall down again to the ground. I will throw one up which shall not come back"; and, dipping into his pocket, he took out the bird and threw it into the air. The bird, rejoicing in its freedom, flew straight up, and then far away, and did not return. "How does that little affair please you, comrade?" asked the tailor.

"You can throw well, certainly," replied the giant; "now let us see if you are in trim to carry something out of the common." So saying, he led him to a huge oak tree, which lay upon the ground, and said, "If you are strong enough, just help me to carry this tree out of the forest."

"With all my heart," replied the tailor; "do you take the trunk upon your shoulder, and I will raise the boughs and branches which are the heaviest, and carry them."

The giant took the trunk upon his shoulder, but the

tailor placed himself on the branch, so that the giant, who was not able to look round, was forced to carry the whole tree and the tailor besides. He, being behind, was very merry, and chuckled at the trick, and presently began to whistle the song, "There rode three tailors out at the gate," as if the carrying of trees were child's play. The giant, after he had staggered along a short distance with his heavy burden, could go no further, and shouted out, "Do you hear? I must let the tree fall." The tailor, springing down, quickly embraced the tree with both arms, as if he had been carrying it, and said to the giant, "Are you such a big fellow, and yet cannot you carry this tree by yourself?"

Then they journeyed on further, and as they came to a cherry tree, the giant seized the top of the tree where the ripest fruits hung, and, bending it down, gave it to the tailor to hold, bidding him eat. But the tailor was much too weak to hold the tree down, and when the giant let go, the tree flew up into the air, and the tailor was carried with it. He came down on the other side, however, without injury, and the giant said, "What does that mean? Have you not strength enough to hold that twig?" "My strength did not fail me," replied the tailor; "do you suppose that that was any hard thing for one who has killed seven at one blow? I have sprung over the tree because the hunters were shooting below there in the thicket. Spring after me if you can." The giant made the attempt, but could not clear the tree, and stuck fast in the branches; so that in this affair, too, the tailor was the better man.

After this the giant said, "Since you are such a valiant fellow, come with me to our house, and stop a night with us." The tailor consented, and followed him; and when they entered the cave, there sat by the fire two other giants, each having a roast sheep in his hand, of which he was eating. The tailor sat down thinking, "Ah, this is much more like the world than is my workshop." And soon the giant showed him a bed where he might lie down and go to sleep. The bed, however, was too big for him, so he slipped out of it, and crept into a corner. When midnight came, and the giant thought the tailor would be in a deep sleep, he got up, and, taking a great iron bar, beat the bed right through at one stroke, and supposed he had thereby given the tailor his death-blow. At the earliest dawn of morning the giants went forth into the forest, quite forgetting the tailor, when presently up he came, quite merry, and showed himself before them. The giants were terrified, and, fearing he would kill them all, they ran away in great haste.

The tailor journeyed on, always following his nose, and after he had wandered some long distance, he came into the courtyard of a royal palace; and as he felt rather tired he laid himself down on the grass and went to sleep. Whilst he lay there the people came and viewed him on all sides, and read upon his belt, "Seven at one blow." "Ah," said they, "what does this great warrior here in time of peace? This must be some mighty hero?" So they went and told the King, thinking that, should war break out, here was an important and useful man, whom one ought not to part with at any price. The King took counsel, and sent one of his courtiers to the tailor to ask for his fighting services, if he should be awake. The messenger stopped at the sleeper's side, and waited till he stretched out his limbs and opened his eyes, and then he laid before him his message. "Solely on that account did I come here," was the reply; "I am quite ready to enter into the King's service." Then he was conducted away with great honour, and a fine house was appointed him to dwell in.

The courtiers, however, became jealous of the tailor, and wished he were a thousand miles away. "What will happen?" said they to one another. "If we go to battle with him, when he strikes out seven will fall at one blow, and nothing will be left for us to do." In their rage they came to the resolution to resign, and they went all together to the King, and asked his permission, saying, "We are not prepared to keep company with a man who kills seven at one blow." The King was grieved to lose all his faithful servants for the sake of one, and wished that he had never seen the tailor, and would willingly have now been rid of him. He dared not, however, dismiss him, because he feared the tailor would kill him and all his subjects, and place himself upon the throne. For a long time he deliberated, till at last he came to a decision; and, sending for the tailor, he told him that, seeing he was so great a hero, he wished to ask a favour of him. "In a certain forest in my kingdom," said the King, "there live two giants, who, by murder, rapine, fire and robbery, have committed great havoc, and no one dares to approach them without perilling his own life. If you overcome and kill both these giants, I will give you my only daughter in marriage, and the half of my kingdom for a dowry; a hundred knights shall accompany you, too, in order to render you assistance."

"Ah, that is something for such a man as I," thought the tailor to himself; "a beautiful Princess and half a kingdom are not offered to one every day." "Oh, yes," he replied, "I will soon manage these two giants, and a hundred horsemen are not necessary for that purpose; he who kills seven at one blow need not fear two."

Thus talking, the little tailor set out, followed by the hundred knights, to whom he said, as soon as they came to the borders of the forest, "Do you stay here; I would rather meet these giants alone." Then he sprang off into the forest, peering about him right and left; and after a while he saw the two giants lying asleep under a tree, snoring so loudly that the branches above them shook violently. The tailor, full of courage, filled both his pockets with stones and clambered up the tree. When he got to the middle of it he crept along a bough, so that he sat just above the sleepers, and then he let fall one stone after another upon the breast of one of them. For some time the giant did not stir, until, at last awaking, he pushed his companion, and said, "Why are you beating me?"

"You are dreaming," he replied; "I never hit you." They laid themselves down again to sleep, and presently the tailor threw a stone down upon the other. "What is that?" he exclaimed. "What are you knocking me for?"

"I did not touch you; you must dream," replied the first. So they wrangled for a few minutes; but, being both very tired with their day's work, they soon fell asleep again. Then the tailor began his sport again, and, picking out the biggest stone, threw it with all his force upon the breast of the first giant. "That is too bad!" he exclaimed; and, springing up like a madman, he fell upon his companion, who, feeling himself equally aggrieved, they set to in such good earnest, that they rooted up trees and beat one another about until they both fell dead upon the ground. Now the tailor jumped down, saying, "What a piece of luck they did not uproot the tree on which I sat, or else I must have jumped on another like a squirrel, for I am not given to flying." Then he drew his sword, and, cutting a deep wound in the breast of each, he went to the horsemen, and said, "The deed is done; I have given each his death-stroke; but it was a hard job, for in their necessity they uprooted trees to defend themselves with; still, all that is of no use when such an one as I come, who killed seven at one stroke."

"Are you not wounded, then?" asked they.

"That is not to be expected; they have not touched a hair of my head," replied the little man. The knights could scarcely believe him, till, riding away into the forest, they found the giants lying in their blood and the uprooted trees around them.

Now the tailor demanded his promised reward of the King; but he repented of his promise, and began to think of some new scheme to get rid of the hero. "Before you receive my daughter and the half of my kingdom," said he to him, "you must perform one other heroic deed. In the forest there runs wild a unicorn, which commits great havoc, and which you must first of all catch."

"I fear still less for a unicorn than I do for two giants! Seven at one blow! that is my motto," said the tailor. Then he took with him a rope and an axe and went away to the forest, bidding those who were ordered to accompany him to wait on the outskirts. He had not to search long, for presently the unicorn came near and prepared to rush at him as if it would pierce him on the spot. "Softly, softly!" he exclaimed; "that is not done so easily"; and, waiting till the animal was close upon him, he sprang nimbly behind a tree. The unicorn, rushing with all its force against the tree, fixed its horn so fast in the trunk, that it could not draw it out again, and so it was made prisoner. "Now I have got my bird," said the tailor; and, coming from behind the tree, he first bound the rope around its neck, and then, cutting the horn out of the tree with his axe, he put all in order, and, leading the animal, brought it before the King.

The King, however, would not yet deliver up the promised reward, and made a third request, that, before the wedding, the tailor should catch a wild boar which did much injury, and he should have the huntsmen to help him. "With pleasure," was the reply, "it is mere child's play." The huntsmen, however, he left behind, to their entire content, for this wild boar had already so often hunted them that they had no pleasure in hunting it. As soon as the boar perceived the tailor, it ran at him with gaping mouth and glistening teeth, and tried to throw him on the ground; but our flying hero sprang into a little chapel which was near, and out again at a window on the other side in a trice. The boar ran after him, but he, skipping round, shut the door behind it, and there the raging beast was caught, for it was much too unwieldy and heavy to jump out of the window. The tailor now called the huntsmen up, that they might see his prisoner with their own eyes; but our hero presented himself before the King, who was compelled now, whether he would or no, to keep his promise, and surrender his daughter and the half of his kingdom.

Had he known that it was no warrior, but only a tailor, who stood before him, it would have gone to his heart still more!

So the wedding was celebrated with great splendour, though with little rejoicing, and out of a tailor was made a King.

Some little while afterwards the young Queen heard her husband talking in his sleep, and saying, "Boy, make me a waistcoat, and stitch up these trousers, or I will lay the yard measure over your ears!" Then she remarked of what condition her lord was, and complained in the morning to her father, and begged he would deliver her from her husband, who was nothing else than a tailor. The King comforted her by saying, "This night leave your chamber door open; my servants shall stand without, and when he is asleep they shall enter, bind him, and bear him away to a ship, which shall carry him forth into the wide world." The wife was contented with his proposal; but the King's armour bearer, who had overheard all, went to the young King and disclosed the whole plot. "I will shoot a bolt upon this affair," said the brave tailor. In the evening at their usual time they went to bed, and when his wife believed he slept she got up, opened the door, and laid herself down again. The tailor, however, only feigned to be asleep, and began to exclaim in a loud voice, "Boy, make me this waistcoat and stitch up these trousers, or I will beat the yard measure about your ears! Seven have I killed with one blow, two giants have I slain, a unicorn have I led captive, and a wild boar have I caught, and shall I be afraid of those who stand without my chamber?" When the men heard these words spoken by the tailor, a great fear overcame them, and they ran away as if the wild huntsmen were behind them; neither afterwards durst any man venture to oppose him. Thus became the tailor a King, and so he remained the rest of his days.

ROLAND

NCE upon a time there lived a real old witch who had two daughters, one ugly and wicked, whom she loved very much, because she was her own child; and the other fair and good, whom she hated, because she was her stepdaughter. One day the stepchild wore a very pretty apron, which so pleased the other that she turned jealous, and told her mother she must and would have the apron. "Be quiet, my child," said she, "you shall have it; your sister has long deserved death. To-night, when she is asleep, I will come and cut off her head; but take care that you lie nearest the wall, and push her quite to the side of the bed."

Luckily the poor maiden, hid in a corner, heard this speech, or she would have been murdered; but all day long she dared not go out of doors, and when bedtime came she was forced to lie in the place fixed for her: but happily the other sister soon went to sleep, and then she contrived to change places and get quite close to the wall. At midnight the old witch sneaked in, holding in her right hand an axe, while with her left she felt for her intended victim; and then raising the axe in both her hands, she chopped off the head of her own daughter.

As soon as she went away, the maiden got up and went to her sweetheart, who was called Roland, and knocked at his door. When he came out she said to him, "Dearest Roland, we must flee at once; my stepmother would have killed me, but in the dark she has murdered her own child; if day comes, and she discovers what she has done, we are lost!"

"But I advise you," said Roland, "first to take away her magic wand, or we cannot save ourselves if she should follow and catch us."

So the maiden stole away the wand, and taking up the head dropped three drops of blood upon the ground: one before the bed, one in the kitchen, and one upon the step; this done, she replaced the head and hurried away with her lover.

When the morning came and the old witch had dressed herself, she called to her daughter and would have given her the apron, but no one came. "Where are you?" she called. "Here upon the step," answered one of the drops of blood. The old woman went out, but seeing nobody on the step, she called a second time, "Where are you?" "Hi, hi, here, in the kitchen; I am warming myself," replied the second drop of blood. She went into the kitchen, but could see nobody; and once again she cried, "Where are you?"

K
N

"Ah! here I sleep in the bed," said the third drop; and she entered the room, but what a sight met her eyes! There lay her own child covered with blood, for she herself had cut off her head.

The old witch flew into a terrible passion, sprang out of the window, and looking far and near, presently spied out her stepdaughter, who was hurrying away with Roland. "That won't help you!" she shouted; "were you twice as far, you should not escape me." So saying, she drew on her boots, in which she went an hour's walk with every stride, and before long she overtook the fugitives. But the maiden, as soon as she saw the witch in sight, changed her dear Roland into a lake with the magic wand, and herself into a duck who could swim upon its surface. When the old witch arrived at the shore, she threw in bread crumbs, and tried all sorts of means to entice the duck; but it was all of no use, and she was obliged to go away at evening without accomplishing her ends. When she was gone the maiden took her natural form, and Roland also, and all night long till daybreak they travelled onwards. Then the maiden changed herself into a rose, which grew amid a very thorny hedge, and Roland became a fiddler. Soon after up came the old witch, and said to him, "Good player, may I break off your flower?" "Oh! yes," he replied, "and I will accompany you with a tune." In great haste she climbed up the bank to reach the flower, and as soon as she was in the hedge he began to play, and, whether she liked it or not, she was obliged to dance to the music, for it was a bewitched tune. The quicker he played, the higher was she obliged to jump, till the thorns tore all the clothes off her body, and scratched and wounded her so much that at last she fell down dead.

Then Roland, when he saw they were saved, said, "Now I will go to my father, and arrange the wedding."

"Yes," said the maiden, "and meanwhile I will rest here, and wait for your return, and, that no one may know me, I will change myself into a red stone."

Roland went away and left her there, but when he reached home he fell into the snares laid for him by another maiden, and forgot his true love, who for a long time waited his coming; but at last, in sorrow and despair of ever seeing him again, she changed herself into a beautiful flower, and thought that perhaps some one might pluck her and carry her to his home.

A day or two after a shepherd, who was tending his flock in the field, chanced to see the enchanted flower; and because it was so very beautiful he broke it off, took it with him, and laid it by in his chest. From that day everything prospered in the shepherd's house, and marvellous things happened. When he arose in the morning he found all the work already done; the room was swept, the chairs and tables dusted, the fire lighted upon the hearth, and the water fetched; when he came home at noonday the table was laid, and a good meal prepared for him. He could not imagine how it was all done, for he could find nobody ever in his house when he returned, and there was no place for any one to conceal himself. The good arrangements certainly pleased him well enough, but he became so anxious at last to know who it was, that he went and asked the advice of a wise woman. The woman said, "There is some witchery in the business; listen one morning if you can hear anything moving in the room, and if you do and can see anything, be it what it will, throw a white napkin over it, and the charm will be dispelled."

The shepherd did as he was bid, and the next morning, just as day broke, he saw his chest open and the flower come out of it. He instantly sprang up and threw a white napkin over it, and immediately the spell was broken, and a beautiful maiden stood before him, who acknowledged that she was the handmaid who, as a flower, had put his house in order. She told him her tale, and she pleased the shepherd so much, that he asked her if she would marry him, but she said, "No," for she would still keep true to her dear Roland, although he had left her; nevertheless, she promised still to remain with the shepherd, and see after his cottage.

Meanwhile, the time had arrived for the celebration of Roland's wedding, and, according to the old custom, it was proclaimed through all the country round, that every maiden might assemble to sing in honour of the bridal pair. When the poor girl heard this, she was so grieved that it seemed as if her heart would break, and she would not have gone to the wedding if others had not come and taken her with them.

When it came to her turn to sing, she stepped back till she was quite by herself, and as soon as she began, Roland jumped up, exclaiming, "I know the voice! that is my true bride! no other will I have!" All that he had hitherto forgotten and neglected to think of was suddenly brought back to his heart's remembrance, and he would not again let her go.

And now the wedding of the faithful maiden to her dear Roland was celebrated with great magnificence; and their sorrows and troubles being over, happiness became their lot.

THE JUNIPER TREE

LONG while ago, perhaps as much as two thousand years, there was a rich man who had a wife of whom he was very fond; but they had no children. Now in the garden, before the house where they lived, there stood a juniper tree; and one winter's day as the lady was standing under the juniper tree, paring an apple, she cut her finger, and the drops of blood trickled down upon the snow. "Ah!" said she, sighing deeply and looking down upon the blood, "how happy should I be if I had a little child as white as snow and as red as blood!" And as she was saying this, she grew quite cheerful, and was sure her wish would be fulfilled. And after a little time the snow went away, and soon afterwards the fields began to look green. Next the spring came, and the meadows were dressed with flowers; the trees put forth their green leaves; the young branches shed their blossoms upon the ground; and the little birds sang through the groves. And then came summer, and the sweet-smelling flowers of the juniper tree began to unfold; and the lady's heart leaped within her, and she fell on her knees for joy.

But when autumn drew near, the fruit was thick upon the trees. Then the lady plucked the red berries from the juniper tree, and looked sad and sorrowful; and she called her husband to her, and said, " If I die, bury me under the juniper tree." Not long after this a pretty little child was born; it was, as the lady wished, as red as blood, and as white as snow; and as soon as she had looked upon it, her joy overcame her, and she fainted away and died.

Then her husband buried her under the juniper tree, and wept and mourned over her; but after a little while he grew better, and at length dried up his tears, and married another wife.

Time passed on, and he had a daughter born; but the child of his first wife, that was as red as blood, and as white as snow, was a little boy. The mother loved her daughter very much, but hated the little boy, and bethought herself how she might get all her husband's money for her own child; so she used the poor fellow very harshly, and was always pushing him about from one corner of the house to another, and thumping him one while and pinching him another, so that he was for ever in fear of her, and when he came home from school could never find a place in the house to play in.

Now it happened that once when the mother was going into her storeroom, the little girl came up to her, and said, " Mother, may I have an apple? " " Yes, my dear," said she, and gave her a nice rosy apple out of the chest. Now you must know that this chest had a very thick heavy lid, with a great sharp iron lock upon it. "Mother," said the little girl, "pray give me one for my little brother too." Her mother did not much like this; however, she said, "Yes, my child; when he comes from school, he shall have one too." As she was speaking, she looked out of the window and saw the little boy coming; so she took the apple from her daughter, and threw it back into the chest and shut the lid, telling her that she should have it again when her brother came home. When the little boy came to the door, this wicked woman said to him with a kind voice, "Come in, my dear, and I will give you an apple." "How kind you are, mother!" said the little boy; "I should like to have an apple very much." "Well, come with me then," said she. So she took him into the store-room and lifted up the cover of the chest, and said, "There, take one out yourself"; and then, as the little boy stooped down to reach one of the apples out of the chest, bang! she let the lid fall, so hard that his head fell off amongst the apples. When she found what she had done, she was very much frightened, and did not know how she should get the blame off her shoulders. However, she went into her bedroom, and took a white handkerchief out of a drawer, and then fitted the little boy's head upon his neck, and tied the handkerchief round it, so that no one could see what had happened, and seated him on a stool before the door with the apple in his hand.

Soon afterwards Margery came into the kitchen to her mother, who was standing by the fire, and stirring about some hot water in a pot. "Mother," said Margery, "my brother is sitting before the door with an apple in his hand; I asked him to give it me, but he did not say a word, and looked so pale, that I was quite frightened." "Nonsense!" said her mother; "go back again, and if he won't answer you, give him a good box on the ear." Margery went back, and said, "Brother, give me that apple." But he answered not a word; so she gave him a box on the ear; and immediately his head fell off. At this, you may be sure she was sadly frightened, and ran screaming out to her mother, that she had knocked off her brother's head, and cried as if her heart would break. "O Margery!" said her mother, "what have you been doing? However, what is done cannot be undone; so we had better put him out of the way, and say nothing to any one about it."

When the father came home to dinner, he said, "Where is my little boy?" And his wife said nothing, but put a large dish of black soup upon the table; and Margery wept bitterly all the time, and could not hold up her head. And the father asked after his little boy again. "Oh!" said his wife, "I should think he is gone to his uncle's." "What business could he have to go away without bidding me good-bye?" said his father. "I know he wished very much to go," said the woman; "and begged me to let him stay there some time; he will be well taken care of there." "Ah!" said the father, "I don't like that; he ought not to have gone away without wishing me good-bye." And with that he began to eat; but he seemed still sorrowful about his son, and said, "Margery, what do you cry so for? your brother will come back again, I hope." But Margery by and by slipped out of the room and went to her drawers and took her best silk handkerchief out of them, and tying it round her little brother's bones, carried them out of the house, weeping bitterly all the while, and laid them under the juniper tree; and as soon as she had done this, her heart felt lighter, and she left off crying. Then the juniper tree began to move itself backwards and forwards, and to stretch its branches out, one from another, and then bring them together again, just like a person clapping hands for joy: and after this, a kind of cloud came from the tree, and in the middle of the cloud was a burning fire, and out of the fire came a pretty bird, that flew away into the air, singing merrily. And as soon as the bird was gone, the handkerchief and the little boy were gone too, and the tree looked just as it had done before; but Margery felt quite happy and joyful within herself, just as if she had known that her brother had been alive again, and went into the house and ate her dinner.

But the bird flew away, and perched upon the roof of a goldsmith's house, and sang:

> " My mother slew her little son ;
> My father thought me lost and gone :
> But pretty Margery pitied me,
> And laid me under the juniper tree ;
> And now I rove so merrily,
> As over the hills and dales I fly :
> O what a fine bird am I ! "

The goldsmith was sitting in his shop finishing a gold chain; and when he heard the bird singing on the house-top, he started up so suddenly that one of his shoes slipped off; however, without stopping to put it on again, he ran out into the street with his apron on, holding his pincers in one hand, and the gold chain in the other. And when he saw the bird sitting on the roof with the sun shining on its bright feathers, he said, "How sweetly you sing, my pretty bird! pray sing that song again." "No," said the bird, "I can't sing twice for nothing; if you will give me that gold chain, I'll try what I can do." "There," said the goldsmith, "take the chain, only pray sing that song again." So the bird flew down, and taking the chain in his right claw, perched a little nearer to the goldsmith, and sang:

> " My mother slew her little son ;
> My father thought me lost and gone :

But pretty Margery pitied me,
And laid me under the juniper tree ;
And now I rove so merrily,
As over the hills and dales I fly :
O what a fine bird am I ! "

After that the bird flew away to a shoemaker's, and sitting upon the roof of the house, sang the same song as it had done before.

When the shoemaker heard the song, he ran to the door without his coat, and looked up to the top of the house; but he was obliged to hold his hand before his eyes, because the sun shone so brightly. "Bird," said he, "how sweetly you sing!" Then he called into the house, "Wife! wife! come out here, and see what a pretty bird is singing on the top of our house!" And he called out his children and workmen; and they all ran out and stood gazing at the bird, with its beautiful red and green feathers, and the bright golden ring about its neck, and eyes which glittered like the stars. "O bird!" said the shoemaker, "pray sing that song again." "No," said the bird, "I cannot sing twice for nothing; you must give me something if I do." "Wife," said the shoemaker, "run upstairs into the workshop, and bring me down the best pair of new red shoes you can find." So his wife ran and fetched them. "Here, my pretty bird," said the shoemaker, "take these shoes; but pray sing that song again." The bird came down, and taking the shoes in his left claw, flew up again to the house-top, and sang:

"My mother slew her little son;
My father thought me lost and gone:
But pretty Margery pitied me,
And laid me under the juniper tree;
And now I rove so merrily,
As over the hills and dales I fly:
O what a fine bird am I!"

And when he had done singing, he flew away, holding the shoes in one claw and the chain in the other. And he flew a long, long way off, till at last he came to a mill. The mill was going clipper! clapper! clipper! clapper! and in the mill were twenty millers, who were all hard at work hewing a millstone; and the millers hewed, hick! hack! hick! hack! and the mill went on, clipper! clapper! clipper! clapper!

So the bird perched upon a linden tree close by the mill, and began its song:

"My mother slew her little son;
My father thought me lost and gone:"

here two of the millers left off their work and listened:

"But pretty Margery pitied me,
And laid me under the juniper tree;"

now all the millers but one looked up and left their work:

"And now I rove so merrily,
As over the hills and dales I fly:
O what a fine bird am I!"

Just as the song was ended, the last miller heard it, and started up, and said, "O bird! how sweetly you sing! do let me hear the whole of that song; pray, sing it again!" "No," said the bird, "I cannot sing twice for nothing; give me that millstone, and I'll sing again." "Why," said the man, "the millstone does not belong to me; if it was all mine, you should have it and welcome." "Come," said the other millers, "if he will only sing that song again, he shall have the millstone." Then the bird came down from the tree: and the twenty millers fetched long poles and worked, and worked, heave, ho! heave, ho! till at last they raised the millstone on its side; and then the bird put its head through the hole in the middle of it, and flew away to the linden tree, and sang the same song as it had done before.

And when he had done, he spread his wings, and with the chain in one claw, and the shoes in the other, and the millstone about his neck, he flew away to his father's house.

Now it happened that his father and mother and Margery were sitting together at dinner. His father was saying, "How light and cheerful I am!" But his mother said, "Oh, I am so heavy and so sad, I feel just as if a great storm were coming on." And Margery said nothing, but sat and cried. Just then the bird came flying along, and perched upon the top of the house. "Bless me!" said the father, "how cheerful I am; I feel as if I was about to see an old friend again." "Alas!" said the mother, "I am so sad, and my teeth chatter so, and yet it seems as if my blood was all on fire in my veins!" and she tore open her gown to cool herself. And Margery sat by herself in a corner, with her plate on her lap before her, and wept so bitterly that she cried her plate quite full of tears.

And the bird flew to the top of the juniper tree and sang:

" My mother slew her little son ;—"

Then the mother held her ears with her hands, and shut her eyes close, that she might neither see nor hear; but there was a sound in her ears like a frightful storm, and her eyes burned and glared like lightning.

" My father thought me lost and gone :—"

" O wife!" said the father, " what a beautiful bird that is, and how finely he sings; and his feathers glitter in the sun like so many spangles!"

" But pretty Margery pitied me,
And laid me under the juniper tree ;—"

At this Margery lifted up her head and sobbed sadly, and her father said, " I must go out, and look at that bird a little nearer." " Oh! don't leave me alone," said his wife; " I feel just as if the house were burning." However, he would go out to look at the bird; and it went on singing:

" But now I rove so merrily,
As over the hills and dales I fly :
O what a fine bird am I!"

As soon as the bird had done singing, he let fall the gold chain upon his father's neck, and it fitted so nicely that he went back into the house and said, "Look here, what a beautiful chain the bird has given me; only see how grand it is!" But his wife was so frightened that she fell all along on the floor, so that her cap flew off, and she lay as if she were dead. And when the bird began singing again, Margery said, "I must go out and see whether the bird has not something to give me." And just as she was going out of the door, the bird let fall the red shoes before her; and when she had put on the shoes, she all at once became quite light and happy, and jumped into the house and said, "I was so heavy and sad when I went out, and now I'm so happy! see what fine shoes the bird has given me!" Then the mother said, "Well, if the world should fall to pieces, I must go out and try whether I shall not be better in the air." And as she was going out, the bird let fall the millstone upon her head and crushed her to pieces.

The father and Margery hearing the noise ran out, and saw nothing but smoke and fire and flame rising up from the place; and when this was passed and gone, there stood the little boy beside them; and he took his father and Margery by the hand, and they went into the house, and ate their dinner together very happily.

RAPUNZEL

NCE upon a time there lived a man and his wife, who much wished to have a child, but for a long time in vain. These people had a little window in the back part of their house, out of which one could see into a beautiful garden which was full of fine flowers and vegetables; but it was surrounded by a high wall, and no one dared to go in, because it belonged to a witch who possessed great power, and who was feared by the whole world. One day the woman stood at this window looking into the garden, and there she saw a bed which was filled with the most beautiful radishes, and which seemed so fresh and green that she felt quite glad, and a great desire seized her to eat of these radishes. This wish tormented her daily, and as she knew that she could not have them she fell ill, and looked very pale and miserable. This frightened her husband, who asked her, "What ails you, my dear wife?"

"Ah!" she replied, "if I cannot get any of those radishes to eat out of the garden behind the house I shall die!" The husband, loving her very much, thought,

"Rather than let my wife die, I must fetch her some radishes, cost what they may." So, in the gloom of the evening, he climbed the wall of the witch's garden, and, snatching a handful of radishes in great haste, brought them to his wife, who made herself a salad with them, which she relished extremely. However, they were so nice and so well-flavoured that the next day after she felt the same desire for the third time, and could not get any rest, so that her husband was obliged to promise her some more. So, in the evening, he made himself ready, and began clambering up the wall; but, oh! how terribly frightened he was, for there he saw the old witch standing before him. "How dare you," she began, looking at him with a frightful scowl, "how dare you climb over into my garden to take away my radishes like a thief? Evil shall happen to you for this."

"Ah!" replied he, "let pardon be granted before justice; I have only done this from a great necessity; my wife saw your radishes from her window, and took such a fancy to them that she would have died if she had not eaten of them." Then the witch ran after him in a passion, saying, "If she behave as you say, I will let you take away all the radishes you please, but I make one condition; you must give me the child which your wife will bring into the world. All shall go well with it, and I will care for it like a mother." In his anxiety the man consented, and when the child was born the witch

K
N

appeared at the same time, gave the child the name "Rapunzel," and took it away with her.

Rapunzel grew to be the most beautiful child under the sun, and when she was twelve years old the witch shut her up in a tower, which stood in a forest, and had neither stairs nor door, and only one little window just at the top. When the witch wished to enter, she stood beneath, and called out:

"Rapunzel! Rapunzel!
Let down your hair."

For Rapunzel had long and beautiful hair, as fine as spun gold; and as soon as she heard the witch's voice she unbound her tresses, opened the window, and then the hair fell down twenty ells, and the witch mounted up by it.

After a couple of years had passed away it happened that the King's son was riding through the wood, and came by the tower. There he heard a song so beautiful that he stood still and listened. It was Rapunzel, who, to pass the time of her loneliness away, was exercising her sweet voice. The King's son wished to ascend to her, and looked for a door in the tower, but he could not find one. So he rode home, but the song had touched his heart so much that he went every day to the forest and listened to it; and as he thus stood one day behind a tree, he saw the witch come up and heard her call out:

"Rapunzel! Rapunzel!
Let down your hair."

Then Rapunzel let down her tresses, and the witch mounted up. "Is that the ladder on which one must climb? Then I will try my luck too," said the Prince; and the following day, as he felt quite lonely, he went to the tower, and said:

"Rapunzel! Rapunzel!
Let down your hair."

Then the tresses fell down, and he climbed up. Rapunzel was much frightened at first when a man came in, for she had never seen one before; but the King's son talked in a loving way to her, and told how his heart had been so moved by her singing that he had no peace until he had seen her himself. So Rapunzel lost her terror, and when he asked her if she would have him for a husband, and she saw that he was young and handsome, she thought, "Any one may have me rather than the old woman." So, saying "Yes," she put her hand within his: "I will willingly go with you, but I know not how I am to descend. When you come, bring with you a skein of silk each time, out of which I will weave a ladder, and when it is ready I will come down by it, and you must take me upon your horse." Then they agreed that they should never meet till the evening, as the witch came in the daytime. The old woman remarked nothing about it, until one day Rapunzel innocently said, " Tell me, mother, how it happens you find it more difficult to come up to me than the young King's son, who is with me in a moment! "

" Oh, you wicked child! " exclaimed the witch, " what do I hear? I thought I had separated you from all the world, and yet you have deceived me." And, seizing Rapunzel's beautiful hair in a fury, she gave her a couple of blows with her left hand, and, taking a pair of scissors in her right, snip, snap, she cut off all her beautiful tresses, and they fell upon the ground. Then she was so hard-hearted that she took the poor maiden into a great desert, and left her to die in great misery and grief.

But the same day when the old witch had carried Rapunzel off, in the evening she made the tresses fast above to the window-latch, and when the King's son came, and called out:

" Rapunzel! Rapunzel!
Let down your hair,"

she let them down. The Prince mounted; but when he got to the top he found, not his dear Rapunzel, but the witch, who looked at him with furious and wicked eyes. " Aha! " she exclaimed, scornfully, " you would fetch your dear wife; but the beautiful bird sits no longer in her nest, singing; the cat has taken her away, and will now scratch out your eyes. To you Rapunzel is lost; you will never see her again."

The Prince lost his senses with grief at these words, and sprang out of the window of the tower in his bewilderment. His life he escaped with, but the thorns into which he fell put out his eyes. So he wandered blind, in the forest, eating nothing but roots and berries, and doing nothing but weep and lament for the loss of his dear wife. He wandered about thus, in great misery, for some few years, and at last arrived at the desert where Rapunzel, with her twins, a boy and a girl, which had been born, lived in great sorrow. Hearing a voice which he thought he knew he followed in its direction, and, as he approached, Rapunzel recognised him and fell upon his neck and wept. Two of her tears moistened his eyes, and they became clear again, so that he could see as well as formerly.

Then he led her away to his kingdom, where he was received with great demonstrations of joy, and where they lived long, contented and happy.

What became of the old witch no one ever knew.

THE THREE MAGIC GIFTS

THE THREE MAGIC GIFTS

LONG time ago, there lived a tailor who had three sons and one goat. As the goat had to feed them all with its milk, it was necessary that it should have good fodder and be taken out to the meadow to graze every day. The sons took it in turns to go with the goat. Once the eldest led it to the churchyard, where the best herbs grew, and let it graze and jump about there. In the evening, when it was time to come home, he asked, "Are you satisfied, goat?"

The goat answered:

> "I am so full,
> Another leaf I could not eat.
> Bleat! bleat!"

"So come home," said the boy; and he put a cord round his neck and led him away and tied him up in the stable.

"Did the goat have its right fodder, and enough?" asked the tailor.

"Oh, yes," answered the son. "She is so full she couldn't eat another leaf."

The father, however, wanted to convince himself, so he went to the stable, stroked his pet, and asked, "Goat, are you full?"

The goat replied:

> "How should I be full?
> Grazing on the graves,
> With not a leaf to eat?
> Bleat! bleat!"

"What do I hear?" cried the tailor; and he ran out and said to the boy, "You wicked boy! you said the goat was full, and instead you have let her starve." And in his wrath he took the yard measure, and with a shower of blows drove him out.

The next day it was the second son's turn to take the goat out. He sought a place in the garden hedge where there were some tasty herbs and weeds; the goat stripped the hedge, and when it was evening and time to go home, he asked, "Goat, are you full?"

The goat answered:

> "I am so full,
> Another leaf I could not eat.
> Bleat! bleat!"

"So come home, then," said the boy. He led him away, and tied him up in the stable.

"Now, then," asked the old tailor, "has the goat had its proper food?"

"Oh," answered the son, "she is so full she couldn't eat another leaf."

But the tailor wasn't satisfied, and he went into the stable and asked, "Goat, are you full?"

The goat replied:

> "How should I be full?
> Grazing on the graves,
> With not a leaf to eat?
> Bleat! bleat!"

"The wicked rascal," cried the tailor, "to let a good animal like this starve!" And with the yard measure he struck his son and drove him off.

It was the third son's turn the next day, and to be quite sure the goat should have good food, he selected a beautiful shrub and let the goat eat the leaves. When evening came and it was time to go home, he asked, "Goat, are you full?"

The goat answered:

> "I am so full,
> Another leaf I could not eat.
> Bleat! bleat!"

"Then come home," said the boy. He led the goat into the stable and tied it up.

"Now, then," said the tailor, "has the goat had its proper food?"

"Oh, yes," answered the son. "She is so full she hasn't room for another leaf."

The tailor didn't trust his word, and went again to the goat and asked, "Goat, are you really full?"

The wicked animal answered:

" How should I be full ?
Grazing on the graves,
With not a leaf to eat ?
Bleat ! bleat ! "

"Oh, you scamp!" exclaimed the tailor, "as bad and undutiful as your brothers. You shan't make a fool of me any longer"; and quite beside himself with anger, he thrashed the poor boy with the yard measure so terribly that he ran away.

The old tailor was now left alone with the goat. The next morning he went to the stable, caressed the goat, and said, "Now, my pretty animal, I will myself take you out to graze." He put the cord round its neck, and led it to a hedge where there were nettles and other things goats like. "Eat to your heart's content," he said, and he let her graze till evening. Then he asked, "Goat, are you full?"

And she answered:

" I am so full,
Another leaf I could not eat.
Bleat ! bleat ! "

"Then come home," said the tailor, and led her into the stable and tied her up. As he was going away he turned round and said, "For once you are full."

But the goat called out as usual:

" How should I be full ?
Grazing on the graves,
With not a leaf to eat ?
Bleat ! bleat ! "

On hearing this the tailor knew the truth, and how he had turned out his three sons without just cause. "Wait a minute," he cried. "You ungrateful brute! to chase you away is not sufficient punishment; I will brand you first, so that you 'll be ashamed to show yourself among honest tailors." He ran and fetched his razor, soaped the goat's head, then shaved it as smooth as his hand. And because the yard measure seemed too honourable a weapon, he seized the whip instead, and lashed the goat till she bounded off in terror.

The tailor, all alone in his house, moped and fell into a melancholy condition. Gladly would he have had his sons back, but he had no idea what had become of them.

The eldest became apprenticed to a carpenter; he served his time diligently, and when his time was up, his master made him a present of a little table, which was made of ordinary wood, but had one peculiarity. If you put it down anywhere and said, "Little table, lay yourself," the good little table was at once covered with a clean cloth, a plate, knife and fork, dishes with boiled and roast meat, and a big bumper of red wine that did your heart good to look at, it sparkled so. The young fellow thought, "With this you will live in plenty all your life," and went to see the world, never troubling about whether an inn were good or bad. If it did not please him he didn't go in, but took his table into a wood or a meadow, or to any spot he fancied. Directly he put it down and said, " Lay yourself," everything was on it that his heart could desire.

At last it occurred to him to go back to his father, whose wrath by this time was sure to have died down, and who would welcome him if he came with the wonderful little table on his back.

It happened that while he was on the way he came to an inn that was filled with guests; they bade him welcome, and invited him to sit down with them to dinner, otherwise he would stand a poor chance of getting anything, as the inn was full.

" No," answered the carpenter, " I will not rob you of a mouthful; on the contrary, I should like to entertain you as my guests."

They laughed, and thought he was joking.

He, however, put down his wooden table in the middle of the room, and said, " Little table, lay yourself." Immediately it was covered with good things to eat, far better than anything the host could supply, and the smell of which seemed very appetising to the guests.

" Set to work, dear friends," said the carpenter; and the guests, when they saw he really meant it, did not wait to be asked again, but came to the table and plied their knives and forks with a will.

The host stood in a corner and looked on; he

didn't know at all what to make of it, but thought such a cook would be useful in his household.

The carpenter and the company he entertained were lively till midnight; then they went to bed, and the young apprentice placed his table against the wall before he lay down to sleep. The host's thoughts were busy meanwhile, and he could not rest for thinking of an old table in the lumber room that looked very much the same as this magic one. At last he went and brought it, and changed it with the carpenter's.

The next morning the carpenter paid his bill, packed up his dear table, little dreaming it was the wrong one, and went his way.

About midday he arrived at his father's, who received him with joyous greetings.

"My dear son, tell me what you've been doing," he said.

"Father, I have become a carpenter."

"A good trade; but what have you brought away as a specimen of your craft?"

"Father, the best thing I could bring was this table."

The tailor examined the table in every part, then said, "I can't say it is a masterpiece; it strikes me as being a very old and a badly made table."

"But," said the son, "it is a table that lays itself; I have only to place it somewhere and to tell it to lay itself, and it produces on the instant dainty dishes and delicious wine. Just invite all your friends and relatives to come and regale themselves; the table will send them away well filled and happy."

When the company arrived, he placed the small table in the middle of the room and said, "Little table, lay yourself," but the table did not stir, and remained as empty as any other table which did not understand language. Then the poor fellow discovered that the table had been changed, and hung his head in shame. The relatives laughed and made game of him, and they were obliged to take their way home unfed and without drinking anything. His father brought out his work again, and tailored away, and the poor son went to find employment in the service of a new master.

The second son meanwhile had gone as apprentice to a miller. When his year was up his master said, "You have worked and behaved so well, that I will give you a present of a donkey of a peculiar kind; he cannot draw a cart or carry any sacks."

"What use is he, then?" asked the young apprentice.

"He spits gold," answered the miller. "If you put him on a cloth and say, 'Bricklebrit,' the good animal will spit out gold coins before and behind."

"Good business," said the apprentice, thanked his master, and went out into the world. When he wanted money he had only to remark "Bricklebrit" to his donkey, and there was a shower of gold coins; so that he had no need to work for a living. Wherever he went he drew the line at nothing. The dearer things were the better, because his purse was always full.

After wandering for some time seeing the world, he thought at last, "It 's time you looked up your father again. If you return home with the gold donkey he will forget his anger and welcome you home."

Now it happened that on the way he put up at the same inn where his brother's table had been changed. He led his donkey by the hand, and his host wanted to take it from him and tie it up, but the young apprentice said, "Don't trouble, please; I will take my grey steed myself into the stable and fasten him up, so that I shall know exactly where he is."

The host thought this curious, and was of opinion that a man who insisted on stabling his own donkey probably hadn't much to spend. However, when his guest put his hand in his pocket and, drawing forth two sovereigns, asked him to bring in a supply of good fare, he opened his eyes with surprise, then ran and procured the best that was to be had.

After the meal the stranger asked how much he had still to pay, and the host, to make as much out of him as possible, said, "Two sovereigns more."

The apprentice put his hand in his pocket, but found his supply of gold had run out. "Wait a minute, landlord," he said, "I will go and fetch more money," and he took the tablecloth with him. The host's curiosity was aroused, and he followed on tiptoe. The guest bolted the stable door behind him, but the spy looked through the keyhole and saw him spread the cloth under the donkey. Directly he had exclaimed, "Bricklebrit," the animal begun to spit gold from every part, till the ground was covered.

"Ah!" said the host, "in that way sovereigns are quickly coined! I wouldn't mind possessing such a mint."

The guest paid his bill and retired to bed.

In the night the host sneaked out to his stable, removed the money-making donkey, and put an ordinary donkey in its place.

Early the following morning the apprentice set off with the animal, which he thought was his gold donkey, arriving at noon at his father's house. He received a warm welcome.

"What have you been doing all this time, son?" asked the old man.

"I have learnt to be a miller," he answered.

"And what have you brought as a specimen of your labours?"

"Nothing but a donkey."

"Donkeys are common enough here," said his father. "I would rather it had been a good goat."

"Yes," answered the son, "but this is no common donkey; you have only to say, 'Bricklebrit,' and the animal will spit out for you a cloth full of sovereigns. Invite all the relatives we have to come and make their fortunes."

"That will be greatly to my mind," said the tailor, "and I needn't slave at my needle any longer."

So when all the relatives had come the young miller told them to sit down, and he spread out the cloth and brought the donkey into the room. "Now look out," he said, and shouted, "Bricklebrit," but no gold coins appeared, and it was evident the donkey had no notion of the art of producing them. Not every donkey is so clever.

The poor miller pulled a long face and begged the relatives' pardon. They had to go home as poor as they came; and the poor old man was obliged to drudge with his needle as he had always done, while the youth took a place under another miller.

The third brother had gone to a turner's to learn the trade, and because turning is an artistic calling his was the longest apprenticeship. His brothers wrote and told him the misfortunes which had befallen them, and how the host of the inn at which they had put up had stolen their valuable magic gifts.

Now when the turner had learnt all there was to learn of the business, and was going to travel, his master presented him with a sack, and remarked, "There is a cudgel inside."

"The sack I can rest on; but what good is the cudgel? It will only make the sack heavy."

"Listen," said the master. "If any one threatens you, all you 've to say is, 'Cudgel, jump out of the sack,' and the cudgel will jump out, and will dance on the backs of people so effectively that they will have to lie still and not move for ten days afterwards."

The apprentice thanked him, slung the sack over his shoulder, and whenever anybody came too near, or was in any way offensive, he merely said, "Cudgel, jump out of the sack," and the cudgel came out and laid about with a will on the backs of the rascals.

The young turner came one evening to the same inn where his brothers had been swindled. He laid his wares on the table, and began to relate stories of the wonderful things he had seen on his travels. "Yes," he said, "it 's all very well to talk about tables that cover themselves, and donkeys that coin sovereigns, but I have a treasure in my sack compared with which these things are nothing at all."

The host pricked up his ears and thought, "The sack is full of precious stones, I 'll be bound. I 'll get it cheaply; all good things come in threes."

When it was time to retire the turner stretched himself on a form, using the sack as a pillow. The host, thinking the guest was in a deep slumber, crept up and began looking at the sack to see if he could pull

it from under the sleeper's head and exchange it for another.

The turner, however, had long been on the look-out, and just as the host had made up his mind to give him a shove and take the sack, he cried, "Cudgel, come out!" Immediately the cudgel jumped forth on to the host's body, which he first scraped, according to a little custom of his, and then began to flog.

The host screamed for mercy, but all the lustier was the cudgel in beating time on his back, till at last the victim fell exhausted on the floor.

The turner then said, "If you will not restore to me the magic table and the gold donkey of which you robbed my brothers, the dance shall begin all over again."

"Ah, no, please," cried the host in a faint voice. "I will restore everything if you will only tell this wretched thing to get back in the sack."

"I will be gracious and show mercy, now justice has been done," said the turner, "but take care what you do next." He then called out, "Cudgel, jump into the sack, and let the host alone."

The next morning the turner set out, taking with him the magic table and the gold donkey. When he arrived at his father's the old tailor was delighted to see him, and asked what he had learnt while he had been out in the world.

"Dear father," he answered, "I have learnt to be a turner."

"A very artistic trade," remarked the father. "And what have you to show?"

"A most costly article, dear father," replied the son, "a cudgel in a sack."

"What!" exclaimed his father, "a cudgel! You can cut one from any tree you come to."

"But not one like this, dear father. If I say, 'Cudgel, jump out of the sack,' the cudgel jumps out, and leads any one who is not friendly to me a dance, beating him till he lies on the ground crying for mercy. Look, with this cudgel I have got back the table that spread itself, and a gold donkey, which a rascally cheating landlord stole from my brothers. Now summon all our relatives and friends, and let them eat and drink, and fill their pockets with gold sovereigns."

The old tailor looked rather unbelieving, but sent for the relatives.

Then the turner fetched a cloth and led in the gold donkey. He said to his brother, "Now, my dear boy, speak to him."

The miller said, "Bricklebrit," and on the instant gold coins rained into the cloth, and the donkey did not stop till every one had picked up more than he could carry. Next the turner fetched the table and said to the other brother, "Speak to it, dear brother." Scarcely had the carpenter cried, "Little table, spread yourself," than it was covered with the most delicious things to eat. A meal was eaten the like of which had never been known in the tailor's house before, and the relatives remained till late, and were all merry and contented.

The tailor for the future locked up his needle and thread, his yard measure, and his iron, in a cupboard, and lived at his ease with his three sons in comfort and plenty.

CATSKIN

HERE was once a King, whose Queen had hair of the purest gold, and was so beautiful that her match was not to be met with on the whole face of the earth. But this beautiful Queen fell ill, and when she felt that her end drew near, she called the King to her and said, "Vow to me that you will never marry again, unless you meet with a wife who is as beautiful as I am, and who has golden hair like mine." Then when the King in his grief had vowed all she asked, she shut her eyes and died. But the King was not to be comforted, and for a long time never thought of taking another wife. At last, however, his counsellors said, "This will not do; the King must marry again, that we may have a Queen." So messengers were sent far and wide, to seek for a bride who was as beautiful as the late Queen. But there was no Princess in the world so beautiful; and if there had been, still there was not one to be found who had such golden hair. So the messengers came home, and had done all their work for nothing.

Now the King had a daughter who was just as beautiful as her mother, and had the same golden hair. And when she was grown up, the King looked at her and saw that she was just like his late Queen; then he said to his courtiers, "May I not marry my daughter? she is the very image of my dead wife: unless I have her, I shall not find any bride upon the whole earth, and you say there must be a Queen." When the courtiers heard this, they were shocked, and said, "Heaven forbid that a father should marry his daughter! out of so great a sin no good can come." And his daughter was also shocked, but hoped the King would soon give up such thoughts; so she said to him, "Before I marry any one I must have three dresses: one must be of gold like the sun, another must be of shining silver like the moon, and a third must be dazzling as the stars; besides this, I want a mantle of a thousand different kinds of fur put together, to which every beast in the kingdom must give a part of his skin." And thus she thought he would think of the matter no more. But the King made the most skilful workmen in his kingdom weave the three dresses, one as golden as the sun, another as silvery as the moon, and a third shining like the stars; and his hunters were told to hunt out all the beasts in his kingdom and take the finest furs out of their skins: and so a mantle of a thousand furs was made.

When all was ready, the King sent them to her; but she got up in the night when all were asleep, and took three of her trinkets, a golden ring, a golden necklace, and a golden brooch; and packed the three dresses of the sun, moon, and stars up in a nutshell, and wrapped herself up in the mantle of all sorts of fur, and besmeared her face and hands with soot. Then she threw herself upon heaven for help in her need, and went away and journeyed on the whole night, till at last she came to a large wood. As she was very tired, she sat herself down in the hollow of a tree and soon fell asleep; and there she slept on till it was midday; and it happened, that as the King to whom the wood belonged was hunting in it, his dogs came to the tree, and began to snuff about and run round and round, and then to bark. "Look sharp," said the King to the huntsmen, "and see what sort of game lies there." And the huntsmen went up to the tree, and when they came back again said, "In the hollow tree there lies a most wonderful beast, such as we never saw before; its skin seems of a thousand kinds of fur, but there it lies fast asleep." "See," said the King, "if you can catch it alive, and we will take it with us." So the huntsmen took it up, and the maiden awoke and was greatly frightened, and said, "I am a poor child that has neither father nor mother left; have pity on me and take me with you." Then they said, "Yes, Miss Catskin, you will do for the kitchen; you can sweep up the ashes and do things of that sort." So they put her in the coach and took her home to the King's palace.

Then they showed her a little corner under the staircase where no light of day ever peeped in, and said, "Catskin, you may lie and sleep there." And she was sent into the kitchen, and made to fetch wood and water, to blow the fire, pluck the poultry, pick the herbs, sift the ashes, and do all the dirty work.

Thus Catskin lived for a long time very sorrowfully. "Ah! pretty Princess!" thought she, "what will now become of thee!" But it happened one day that a feast was to be held in the King's castle; so she said to the cook, "May I go up a little while and see what is going on? I will take care and stand behind the door." And the cook said, "Yes, you may go, but be back again in half an hour's time to rake out the ashes." Then she took her little lamp, and went into her cabin, and took off the fur skin, and washed the soot from off her face and hands, so that her beauty shone forth like the sun from behind the clouds. She next opened her nutshell, and brought out of it the dress that shone like the sun, and so went to the feast. Every one made way for her, for nobody knew her, and they thought she could be no less than a King's daughter. But the King came up to her and held out his hand and danced with her, and he thought in his heart, "I never saw any one half so beautiful."

When the dance was at an end, she curtsied; and when the King looked round for her she was gone, no one knew whither. The guards who stood at the castle gate were called in; but they had seen no one. The truth was, that she had run into her little cabin, pulled off her dress, blacked her face and hands, put on the fur-skin cloak, and was Catskin again. When she went into the kitchen to her work, and began to rake the ashes, the cook said, "Let that alone till the morning, and heat the King's soup; I should like to run up now and give a peep; but take care you don't let a hair fall into it, or you will run a chance of never eating again."

As soon as the cook went away, Catskin heated the King's soup and toasted up a slice of bread as nicely as ever she could; and when it was ready, she went and looked in the cabin for her little golden ring, and put it into the dish in which the soup was. When the dance was over, the King ordered his soup to be brought in, and it pleased him so well that he thought he had never tasted any so good before. At the bottom he saw a gold ring lying, and as he could not make out how it had got there, he ordered the cook to be sent for. The cook was frightened when she heard the order, and said to Catskin, "You must have let a hair fall into the soup; if it be so, you will have a good beating." Then she went before the King, and he asked her who had cooked the soup. "I did," answered she. But the King said, "That is not true; it was better done than you could do it."

Then she answered, " To tell the truth, I did not cook it, but Catskin did." " Then let Catskin come up," said the King; and when she came, he said to her, "Who are you?" " I am a poor child," said she, " who has lost both father and mother." " How came you in my palace? " asked he. " I am good for nothing," said she, " but to be scullion girl, and to have boots and shoes thrown at my head." " But how did you get the ring that was in the soup? " asked the King. But she would not own that she knew anything about the ring; so the King sent her away again about her business.

After a time there was another feast, and Catskin asked the cook to let her go up and see it as before. " Yes," said she, " but come back again in half an hour, and cook the King the soup that he likes so much." Then she ran to her little cabin, washed herself quickly, and took the dress out which was silvery as the moon, and put it on; and when she went in looking like a King's daughter, the King went up to her and rejoiced at seeing her again, and when the dance began he danced with her. After the dance was at an end, she managed to slip out so slyly that the King did not see where she was gone; but she sprang into her little cabin and made herself into Catskin again, and went into the kitchen to cook the soup. Whilst the cook was above, she got the golden necklace, and dropped it into the soup; then it was brought to the King, who ate it, and it pleased him as well as before; so he sent for the cook, who was again forced to tell him that Catskin had cooked it. Catskin was brought again before the King; but she still told him that she was only fit to have the boots and shoes thrown at her head.

But when the King had ordered a feast to be got ready for the third time, it happened just the same as before. "You must be a witch, Catskin," said the cook; "for you always put something into the soup, so that it pleases the King better than mine." However, she let her go up as before. Then she put on the dress which sparkled like the stars, and went into the ballroom in it; and the King danced with her again, and thought she had never looked so beautiful as she did then: so whilst he was dancing with her, he put a gold ring on her finger without her seeing it, and ordered that the dance should be kept up a long time. When it was at an end, he would have held her fast by the hand; but she slipped away and sprang so quickly through the crowd that he lost sight of her; and she ran as fast as she could into her little cabin under the stairs. But this time she kept away too long, and stayed beyond the half hour; so she had not time to take off her fine dress, but threw her fur mantle over it, and in her haste did not soot herself all over, but left one finger white.

Then she ran into the kitchen, and cooked the King's soup; and as soon as the cook was gone, she put the golden brooch into the dish. When the King got to the bottom, he ordered Catskin to be called once more, and soon saw the white finger and the ring that he had put on it whilst they were dancing; so he seized her hand, and kept fast hold of it, and when she wanted to loose herself and spring away, the fur cloak fell off a little on one side, and the starry dress sparkled underneath it. Then he got hold of the fur and tore it off, and her golden hair and beautiful form were seen, and she could no longer hide herself; so she washed the soot and ashes from off her face, and showed herself to be the most beautiful Princess upon the face of the earth. But the King said, "You are my beloved bride, and we will never more be parted from each other." And the wedding feast was held, and a merry day it was.

THE GOLDEN GOOSE

THE GOLDEN GOOSE

HERE was a man who had three sons. The youngest was called Dummling, and was on all occasions despised and ill-treated by the whole family. It happened that the eldest took it into his head one day to go into the wood to cut fuel; and his mother gave him a delicious pasty and a bottle of wine to take with him, that he might refresh himself at his work. As he went into the wood, a little old man bid him good day, and said, "Give me a little piece of meat from your plate, and a little wine out of your bottle; I am very hungry and thirsty." But this clever young man said, "Give you my meat and wine! No, I thank you; I should not have enough left for myself": and away he went. He soon began to cut down a tree; but he had not worked long before he missed his stroke, and cut himself, and was obliged to go home to have the wound dressed. Now it was the little old man that caused him this mischief.

Next went out the second son to work; and his

mother gave him too a pasty and a bottle of wine. And the same little old man met him also, and asked him for something to eat and drink. But he too thought himself vastly clever, and said, "Whatever you get, I shall lose; so go your way!" The little man took care that he should have his reward; and the second stroke that he aimed against a tree, hit him on the leg; so that he too was forced to go home.

Then Dummling said, "Father, I should like to go and cut wood too." But his father answered, "Your brothers have both lamed themselves; you had better stay at home, for you know nothing of the business." But Dummling was very pressing; and at last his father said, "Go your way; you will be wiser when you have suffered for your folly." And his mother gave him only some dry bread, and a bottle of sour beer; but when he went into the wood, he met the little old man, who said, "Give me some meat and drink, for I am very hungry and thirsty." Dummling said, "I have only dry bread and sour beer; if that will suit you, we will sit down and eat it together." So they sat down; and when the lad pulled out his bread, behold it was turned into a capital pasty, and his sour beer became delightful wine. They ate and drank heartily; and when they had done, the little man said, "As you have a kind heart, and have been willing to share everything with me, I will send a blessing upon you. There stands an old tree; cut it

K.
N.

down, and you will find something at the root." Then he took his leave, and went his way.

Dummling set to work, and cut down the tree; and when it fell, he found in a hollow under the roots a goose with feathers of pure gold. He took it up, and went on to an inn, where he proposed to sleep for the night. The landlord had three daughters; and when they saw the goose they were very curious to examine what this wonderful bird could be, and wished very much to pluck one of the feathers out of its tail. At last the eldest said, "I must and will have a feather." So she waited till his back was turned, and then seized the goose by the wing; but to her great surprise there she stuck, for neither hand nor finger could she get away again. Presently in came the second sister, and thought to have a feather too; but the moment she touched her sister, there she too hung fast. At last came the third, and wanted a feather; but the other two cried out, "Keep away! for heaven's sake, keep away!" However, she did not understand what they meant. "If they are there," thought she, "I may as well be there too." So she went up to them; but the moment she touched her sisters she stuck fast, and hung to the goose as they did. And so they kept company with the goose all night.

The next morning Dummling carried off the goose under his arm; and took no notice of the three girls, but went out with them sticking fast behind; and wherever he travelled they too were obliged to follow, whether they would or no, as fast as their legs could carry them.

In the middle of a field the parson met them; and when he saw the train, he said, "Are you not ashamed of yourselves, you bold girls, to run after the young man in that way over the fields? is that proper behaviour?" Then he took the youngest by the hand to lead her away; but the moment he touched her he too hung fast, and followed in the train. Presently up came the clerk; and when he saw his master the parson running after the three girls, he wondered greatly, and said, "Hollo! hollo! your reverence! whither so fast? there is a christening to-day." Then he ran up, and took him by the gown, and in a moment he was fast too. As the five were thus trudging along, one behind another, they met two labourers with their mattocks coming from work; and the parson cried out to them to set him free. But scarcely had they touched him, when they too fell into the ranks, and so made seven, all running after Dummling and his goose.

At last they arrived at a city, where reigned a King who had an only daughter. The Princess was of so thoughtful and serious a turn of mind that no one could make her laugh; and the King had proclaimed to all the world, that whoever could make her laugh should have her for his wife. When the young man heard this, he went to her with his goose and all its train; and as soon as she saw the seven all hanging together, and running about, treading on each other's heels, she could not help bursting into a long and loud laugh. Then Dummling claimed her for his wife; the wedding was celebrated, and he was heir to the kingdom, and lived long and happily with his wife.

RUMPELSTILTSKIN

IN a certain kingdom once lived a poor miller who had a very beautiful daughter. She was moreover exceedingly shrewd and clever; and the miller was so vain and proud of her, that he one day told the King of the land that his daughter could spin gold out of straw. Now this King was very fond of money; and when he heard the miller's boast, his avarice was excited, and he ordered the girl to be brought before him. Then he led her to a chamber where there was a great quantity of straw, gave her a spinning-wheel, and said, "All this must be spun into gold before morning, as you value your life." It was in vain that the poor maiden declared that she could do no such thing, the chamber was locked and she remained alone.

She sat down in one corner of the room and began to lament over her hard fate, when on a sudden the door opened, and a droll-looking little man hobbled in, and said, "Good morrow to you, my good lass, what are you weeping for?" "Alas!" answered she, "I must spin this straw into gold, and I know not how." "What will you give me," said the little man, "to do it for you?" "My necklace," replied the maiden. He took her at her word, and sat himself down to the wheel; round about it went merrily, and presently the work was done and the gold all spun.

When the King came and saw this, he was greatly astonished and pleased; but his heart grew still more greedy of gain, and he shut up the poor miller's daughter again with a fresh task. Then she knew not what to do, and sat down once more to weep; but the little man presently opened the door, and said, "What will you give me to do your task?" "The ring on my finger," replied she. So her little friend took the ring, and began to work at the wheel, till by the morning all was finished again.

The King was vastly delighted to see all this glittering treasure; but still he was not satisfied, and took the miller's daughter into a yet larger room, and said, "All this must be spun to-night; and if you succeed, you shall be my Queen." As soon as she was alone the dwarf came in, and said, "What will you give me to spin gold for you this third time?" "I have nothing left," said she. "Then promise me," said the little man, "your first little child when you are Queen." "That may never be," thought the miller's daughter; and as she knew no other way to get her task done, she promised him what he asked, and he spun once more the whole heap of gold. The

King came in the morning, and finding all he wanted, married her, and so the miller's daughter really became Queen.

At the birth of her first little child the Queen rejoiced very much, and forgot the little man and her promise; but one day he came into her chamber and reminded her of it. Then she grieved sorely at her misfortune, and offered him all the treasures of the kingdom in exchange; but in vain, till at last her tears softened him, and he said, "I will give you three days' grace, and if during that time you tell me my name, you shall keep your child."

Now the Queen lay awake all night, thinking of all the odd names that she had ever heard, and despatched messengers all over the land to inquire after new ones. The next day the little man came, and she began with Timothy, Benjamin, Jeremiah, and all the names she could remember; but to all of them he said, "That's not my name."

The second day she began with all the comical names she could hear of, Bandy-legs, Hunch-back, Crook-shanks, and so on, but the little gentleman still said to every one of them, "That's not my name."

The third day came back one of the messengers, and said, "I can hear of no one other name; but yesterday, as I was climbing a high hill among the trees of the forest where the fox and the hare bid each other good night, I saw a little hut, and before the hut burnt a fire, and round about the fire danced a funny little man upon one leg, and sung :

> " Merrily the feast I 'll make,
> To-day I 'll brew, to-morrow bake ;
> Merrily I 'll dance and sing,
> For next day will a stranger bring :
> Little does my lady dream
> Rumpelstiltskin is my name ! "

When the Queen heard this, she jumped for joy, and as soon as her little visitor came, and said, " Now, lady, what is my name ? " " Is it John ? " asked she. " No ! " " Is it Tom ? " " No ! "

> " Can your name be Rumpelstiltskin ? "

"Some witch told you that ! Some witch told you that !" cried the little man, and dashed his right foot in a rage so deep into the floor, that he was forced to lay hold of it with both hands to pull it out. Then he made the best of his way off, while everybody laughed at him for having had all his trouble for nothing.

THE TWO BROTHERS

NCE upon a time there were two brothers, the one rich and the other poor. The rich man was a goldsmith, and of an evil disposition; but the poor brother maintained himself by mending brooms, and withal was honest and pious. He had two children—twins, as like one another as two drops of water—who used often to go into their rich uncle's house and receive a meal off the fragments which he left. One day it happened when the poor man had gone into the wood for twigs that he saw a bird, which was of gold, and more beautiful than he had ever before set eyes on. He picked up a stone and flung it at the bird, and luckily hit it, but so slightly that only a single feather dropped off. This feather he took to his brother, who looked at it and said, "It is of pure gold!" and gave him a good sum of money for it. The next day he climbed up a birch tree to lop off a bough or two, when the same bird flew out of the branches, and as he looked round he found a nest which contained an egg, also of gold. This he took home as before to his brother, who said it was of pure gold, and gave him what it was worth, but said that he must have the bird itself. For the third time now the brother went into the forest, and saw the golden bird sitting again upon the tree, and taking up a stone he threw it at it, and, securing it, took it to his brother, who gave him for it a large pile of gold. With this the man thought he might return, and went home light-hearted.

But the goldsmith was crafty and bold, knowing very well what sort of a bird it was. He called his wife and said to her, "Roast this bird for me, and take care of whatever falls from it, for I have a mind to eat it by myself." Now, the bird was not an ordinary one, certainly, for it possessed this wonderful power, that whoever should eat its heart and liver would find henceforth every morning a gold piece under his pillow. The wife made the bird ready, and putting it on a spit, set it down to roast. Now it happened that while it was at the fire, and the woman had gone out of the kitchen on some other necessary work, the two children of the poor broom-mender ran in, and began to turn the spit round at the fire for amusement. Presently two little titbits fell down into the pan out of the bird, and one of the boys said, "Let us eat these two little pieces, I am so hungry, and nobody will find it out." So they quickly despatched the two morsels, and presently the woman came back, and, seeing at once they had eaten something, asked them what it was. "Two little bits which

The unicorn, rushing against the tree, fixed its horn so fast in the trunk that it could not draw it out. (Page 159)

A kind of cloud came from the tree, and in the middle was a burning fire, and out of the fire came a pretty bird. (Page 179)

fell down out of the bird," was the reply. "They were the heart and liver!" exclaimed the woman, quite frightened; and, in order that her husband might not miss them and be in a passion, she quickly killed a little chicken, and, taking out its liver and heart, put it inside the golden bird. As soon as it was done enough she carried it to the goldsmith, who devoured it quite alone, and left nothing at all on the plate. The next morning, however, when he looked under his pillow, expecting to find the gold pieces, there was not the smallest one possible to be seen.

The two children did not know what good luck had fallen upon them, and, when they got up the next morning, something fell ringing upon the ground, and as they picked it up they found it was two gold pieces. They took them to their father, who wondered very much, and considered what he should do with them; but as the next morning the same thing happened, and so on every day, he went to his brother, and narrated to him the whole story. The goldsmith perceived at once what had happened, that the children had eaten the heart and the liver of his bird; and in order to revenge himself, and because he was so covetous and hard-hearted, he persuaded the father that his children were in league with the devil, and warned him not to take the gold, but to turn them out of the house, for the Evil One had them in his power, and would make them do some mischief. Their father feared the Evil One, and, although it cost him a severe pang, he led his children out in the forest and left them there with a sad heart.

Now, the two children ran about the wood, seeking the road home, but could not find it, so that they only wandered further away. At last they met a huntsman, who asked to whom they belonged. "We are the children of the poor broom-mender," they replied, and told him that their father could no longer keep them at home, because a gold piece lay under their pillows every morning. "Well," replied the huntsman, "that does not seem right, if you are honest and not idle." And the good man, having no children of his own, took home with him the twins, because they pleased him, and told them he would be their father and bring them up. With him they learned all kinds of hunting, and the gold pieces, which each one found at his uprising, they laid aside against a rainy day.

When now they became quite young men the huntsman took them into the forest, and said, "To-day you must perform your shooting trial, that I may make you free huntsmen like myself." So they went with him, and waited a long time, but no wild beast approached, and the huntsman, looking up, saw a flock of wild geese, flying over in the form of a triangle. "Shoot one from each corner," said he to the twins, and when they had done this, another flock came flying over in the form of a figure of two, and from these they were also bid to shoot one at each corner. When they had likewise performed this deed successfully their foster-father said, "I now make you free; for you are capital marksmen."

Thereupon the two brothers went together into the forest, laying plans and consulting with each other; and, when at evening-time they sat down to their meal, they said to their foster-father, "We shall not touch the least morsel of food till you have granted our request."

He asked them what it was, and they replied:

"We have now learned everything; let us go into the world, and see what we can do there, and let us set out at once."

"You have spoken like brave huntsmen," cried the old man, overjoyed; "what you have asked is just what I wished; you can set out as soon as you like, for you will be prosperous."

Then they ate and drank together once more in great joy and hilarity.

When the appointed day arrived, the old huntsman gave to each youth a good rifle and a dog, and let them take from the gold pieces as many as they liked. Then he accompanied them a part of their way, and at leaving gave them a bare knife, saying, "If you should separate, stick this knife in a tree by the roadside, and then, if one returns to the same point, he can tell how his absent brother fares; for the side upon which there is a mark will, if he die, rust; but as long as he lives it will be as bright as ever."

The two brothers now journeyed on till they came to a forest so large that they could not possibly get out of it in one day, so there they passed the night, and ate what they had in their hunters' pockets. The second day they still walked on, but came to no opening, and having nothing to eat, one said, "We must shoot something, or we shall die of hunger"; and he loaded his gun and looked around. Just then an old hare came running up, at which he aimed, but it cried out:

> "Dear huntsman, pray now let me live,
> And I will two young lev'rets give."

So saying, it ran back into the brushwood and brought out two hares, but they played about so prettily and actively that the hunters could not make up their mind to kill them. So they took them with them, and the two leverets followed in their footsteps. Presently a fox came up with them, and, as they were about to shoot it, it cried out:

> "Dear hunters, pray now let me live,
> And I will two young foxes give."

These it brought; and the brothers, instead of killing them, put them with the young hares, and all four followed. In a little while a wolf came out of the brushwood, whom the hunters also aimed at, but he cried out as the others:

" Dear hunters, pray now let me live,
Two young ones, in return, I 'll give."

The hunters placed the two wolves with the other animals, who still followed them; and soon they met a bear, who also begged for his life, saying:

" Dear hunters, pray now let me live,
Two young ones, in return, I 'll give."

These two bears were added to the others: they made eight; and now who came last? A lion, shaking his mane. The two brothers were not frightened, but aimed at him, and he cried:

" Dear hunters, pray now let me live,
Two young ones, in return, I 'll give."

The lion then fetched his two young cubs, and now the huntsmen had two lions, two bears, two wolves, two foxes, and two hares following and waiting upon them. Meanwhile their hunger had received no satisfaction, and they said to the foxes, "Here, you slinks, get us something to eat, for you are both sly and crafty."

The foxes replied, "Not far from here lies a village, where we can procure many fowls, and thither we will show you the way."

So they went into the village, and bought something to eat for themselves and their animals, and then went on further, for the foxes were well acquainted with the country where the hen-roosts were, and so could direct the huntsmen well.

For some little way they walked on without finding any situations where they could live together; so they said to one another, "It cannot be otherwise, we must separate." Then the two brothers divided the beasts, so that each one had a lion, a bear, a wolf, a fox, and a hare; and then they took leave of each other, promising to love one another till death; and the knife which their foster-father gave them they stuck in a tree, so that one side pointed to the east, and the other to the west.

The younger brother came afterwards with his animals to a town which was completely hung with black crape. He went into an inn and inquired if he could lodge his beasts, and the landlord gave him a stable, and in the wall was a hole through which the hare crept and seized upon a cabbage; the fox fetched himself a hen, and when he had eaten it he stole the cock also; but the lion, the bear, and the wolf, being too big for the hole, could get nothing. The master, therefore, made the host fetch an ox for them, on which they regaled themselves merrily, and so, having seen after his beasts, he asked the landlord why the town was all hung in mourning. The landlord replied, it was because the next day the King's only daughter was to die. "Is she then sick unto death?" inquired the huntsman.

"No," replied the other, "she is well enough; but still she must die."

"How is that?" asked the huntsman.

"Out there before the town," said the landlord, "is a high mountain on which lives a dragon, who must every year have a pure maiden, or he would lay waste all the country. Now, all the maidens have been given up, and there is but one left, the King's daughter, who must also be given up, for there is no other escape, and to-morrow morning it is to happen."

The huntsman asked, "Why is the dragon not killed?"

"Ah!" replied the landlord, "many knights have tried, but every one has lost his life; and the King has promised his own daughter to him who conquers the dragon, and after his death the inheritance of his kingdom."

The huntsman said nothing further at that time, but the next morning, taking with him his beasts, he climbed the dragon's mountain. A little way up stood a chapel, and upon an altar therein were three cups, and by them was written, "Whoever drinks the contents of these cups will be the strongest man on earth, and may take the sword which lies buried beneath the threshold." Without drinking, the huntsman sought and found the sword in the ground, but he could not move it from its place; so he entered, and drank out of the cups, and then he easily pulled out the sword, and was so strong that he waved it about like a feather.

When the hour arrived that the maiden should be

delivered over to the dragon, the King and his Marshal accompanied her with all the court. From a distance they perceived the huntsman upon the mountain, and took him for the dragon waiting for them, and so would not ascend; but at last, because the whole city must otherwise have been sacrificed, the Princess was forced to make the dreadful ascent. The King and his courtiers returned home full of grief, but the Marshal had to stop and watch it all from a distance.

As the King's daughter reached the top of the hill she found there not the dragon, but the young hunter, who comforted her, saying he would save her, and, leading her into the chapel, shut her up therein. In a short time the seven-headed dragon came roaring up with a tremendous noise, and, as soon as he perceived the hunter, he was amazed, and asked, "What do you here on my mountain?"

The hunter replied that he came to fight him, and the dragon said, breathing out fire as he spoke from his seven jaws, "Many a knight has already left his life behind him, and you I will soon kill as dead as they." The fire from his throat set the grass in a blaze, and would have suffocated the hunter with the smoke had not his beasts come running up and stamped it out. Then the dragon made a dart at the hunter, but he swung his sword round so that it whistled in the air, and cut off three of the beast's heads. The dragon now became furious and raised himself in the air, spitting out fire over his enemy, and trying to overthrow him; but the hunter, springing on one side, raised his sword again, and cut off three more of his heads. The beast was half killed with this, and sank down, but tried once more to catch the hunter, but he beat him off, and, with his last strength, cut off his tail; and then, being unable to fight longer, he called his beasts, who came and tore the dragon in pieces.

As soon as the battle was over he went to the chapel and unlocked the door, and found the Princess lying on the floor; for, from anguish and terror, she had fainted away while the contest was going on. The hunter carried her out, and when she came to herself and opened her eyes, he showed her the dragon torn to pieces, and said she was now safe for ever. The sight made her quite happy, and she said, "Now you will be my husband, for my father has promised me to him who should kill the dragon." So saying, she took off her necklace of coral, and divided it among the beasts for a reward, the lion receiving the gold snap for his share. But her handkerchief, on which her name was marked, she presented to the huntsman, who went and cut out the tongues of the dragon's seven mouths, and, wrapping them in the handkerchief, preserved them carefully.

All this being done, the poor fellow felt so weary with the battle with the dragon and the fire, that he said to the Princess, " Since we are both so tired, let us sleep awhile." She consented, and they lay down on the ground, and the hunter bid the lion watch that nobody surprised them. Soon they began to snore, and the lion sat down near them to watch: but he was also weary with fighting, and he said to the bear, " Do you lie down near me, for I must sleep a bit; but wake me up if any one comes." So the bear did as he was bid; but soon getting tired, he asked the wolf to watch for him. The wolf consented, but before long he called the fox, and said, " Do watch for me a little while, I want to have a nap, and you can wake me if any one comes." The fox lay down by his side, but soon felt so tired himself that he called the hare, and asked him to take his place and watch while he slept a little. The hare came, and lying down too, soon felt very sleepy; but he had no one to call in his place, so by degrees he dropped off himself, and began to snore. Here, then, were sleeping the Princess, the huntsman, the lion, the bear, the wolf, the fox, and the hare; and all were very sound asleep.

Meanwhile the Marshal, who had been set to watch below, not seeing the dragon fly away with the Princess, and all appearing very quiet, took heart, and climbed up the mountain. There lay the dragon, dead and torn to pieces on the ground, and not far off the King's daughter and a huntsman with his beasts, all reposing in a deep sleep. Now, the Marshal was very wickedly disposed, and, taking his sword, he cut off the head of the huntsman, and then, taking the maiden under his arm, carried her down the mountain. At this she awoke, terrified, and the Marshal cried to her, "You are in my hands; you must say that it was I who have killed the dragon."

"That I cannot," she replied, "for a hunter and his animals did it." Then he drew his sword, and threatened her with death if she did not obey, till at last she was forced to consent. Thereupon he brought her before the King, who went almost beside himself with joy at seeing again his dear daughter, whom he supposed had been torn in pieces by the monster. The Marshal told the King that he had killed the dragon, and freed the Princess and the whole kingdom, and therefore he demanded her for a wife, as it had been promised. The King inquired of his daughter if it were true? "Ah, yes," she replied, "it must be so; but I make a condition, that the wedding shall not take place for a year and a day"; for she thought to herself that perhaps in that time she might hear some news of her dear huntsman.

But up the dragon's mountain the animals still lay asleep beside their dead master, when presently a great bee came and settled on the hare's nose, but he lifted his paw and brushed it off. The bee came a second time, but the hare brushed it off again, and went to sleep. For the third time the bee settled, and stung the hare's nose so that he woke quite up. As soon as he had risen and shaken himself, he awoke the fox, and the fox awoke the wolf, the wolf awoke the bear, and the bear awoke the lion. As soon as the lion got up and saw that the maiden was gone and his dear master dead, he began to roar fearfully, and asked, "Who has done this? Bear, why did you not wake me?" The bear asked the wolf, "Why did you not wake me?" The wolf asked the fox, "Why did you not wake me?" and the fox asked the hare, "Why did you not wake me?" The poor hare alone had nothing to answer, and the blame was attached to him, and the others would have fallen upon him, but he begged for his life, saying, "Do not kill me, and I will restore our dear master to life. I know a hill where grows a root, and he who puts it in his mouth is healed immediately from all diseases or wounds; but this mountain lies two hundred hours' journey from hence."

The lion said, "In four-and-twenty hours you must go and return here, bringing the root with you."

The hare immediately ran off, and in four-and-twenty hours returned with the root in his mouth. Now the lion put the huntsman's head again to his body while the hare applied the root to the wound, and immediately the huntsman began to revive, and his heart beat and life returned. The huntsman now awoke, and was frightened to see the maiden no longer with him, and he thought to himself, " Perhaps she ran away while I slept, to get rid of me." But, in his haste, the lion had unluckily set his master's head on the wrong way, but the hunter did not find it out till midday, when he wanted to eat, being so occupied with thinking about the Princess. Then, when he wished to help himself, he discovered his head was turned to his back, and, unable to imagine the cause, he asked the animals what had happened to him in his sleep. The lion told him that from weariness they had all gone to sleep, and, on awaking, they had found him dead, with his head cut off; that the hare had fetched the life-root, but in his great haste he had turned his head the wrong way, but that he would make it all right again in no time. So saying, he cut off the huntsman's head and turned it round, while the hare healed the wound with the root.

After this the hunter became very mopish, and went about from place to place letting his animals dance to the people for show. It chanced, after a year's time, that he came again into the same town where he had rescued the Princess from the dragon; and this time it was hung all over with scarlet cloth. He asked the landlord of the inn, " What means this? a year ago the city was hung with black crape, and to-day it is all in red!" The landlord replied, "A year ago our King's daughter was delivered to the dragon, but our Marshal fought with it and slew it, and this day their marriage is to be celebrated; before the town was hung with crape in token of grief and lamentation, but to-day with scarlet cloth, to show our joy."

The next day, when the wedding was to take place, the huntsman said to the landlord, "Believe it or not, mine host, but to-day I will eat bread from the table of the King!"

"Well," said he, "I will wager you a hundred pieces that that doesn't come true."

The huntsman took the bet, and laid down his money; and then, calling the hare, he said, "Go, dear Jumper, and fetch me a bit of bread such as the King eats."

Now, the hare was the smallest, and therefore could not entrust his business to any one else, but was obliged to make himself ready to go. "Oh!" thought he, "if I jump along the streets alone, the butchers' dogs will come out after me."

While he stood considering, it happened as he thought; for the dogs came behind and were about to seize him for a choice morsel, but he made a spring (had you but seen it!), and escaped into a sentry-box without the soldier knowing it. The dogs came and tried to hunt him out, but the soldier, not understanding their sport, beat them off with a club, so that they ran howling and barking away. As soon as the hare saw the coast was clear, he ran up to the castle and into the room where the Princess was, and, getting under her stool, began to scratch her foot. The Princess said, "Will you be quiet?" thinking it was her dog. Then the hare scratched her foot a second time, and she said again, "Will you be quiet?" But the hare would not leave off, and a third time scratched her foot; and now she peeped down and recognised the hare by his necklace. She took him up in her arms, and carried him into her chamber. "Dear hare, what do you want?" The hare replied, "My master who killed the dragon is here, and sent me; I am come for a piece of bread such as the King eats."

At these words she became very glad, and bade her servant bring her a piece of bread such as the King was accustomed to have. When it was brought, the hare said, "The baker must carry it for me, or the butchers' dogs will seize it." So the baker carried it to the door of the inn, where the hare got upon his hind legs, and, taking the bread in his forepaws, carried it to his master. Then the huntsman said, "See here, my host; the hundred gold pieces are mine."

The landlord wondered very much, but the huntsman said further, "Yes, I have got the King's bread, and now I will have some of his meat." To this the landlord demurred, but would not bet again; and his guest, calling the fox, said, "My dear fox, go and fetch me some of the meat which the King is to eat to-day."

The fox was more cunning than the hare, and went through the lanes and alleys, without seeing a dog, straight to the royal palace, and into the room of the Princess, under whose stool he crept. Presently he scratched her foot, and the Princess, looking down, recognised the fox with her necklace, and, taking him into her room, she asked, "What do you want, dear fox?" He replied, "My master who killed the dragon is here, and sent me to beg a piece of the meat such as the King will eat to-day."

The Princess summoned the cook, and made her prepare a dish of meat like the King's; and, when it was ready, carry it for the fox to the door of the inn. Then the fox took the dish himself; and, first driving the flies away with a whisk of his tail, carried it in to the hunter.

"See here, Master Landlord," said he; "here are the bread and meat: now I will have the same vegetables as the King eats."

He called the wolf, and said, "Dear wolf, go and fetch me some vegetables the same as the King eats to-day."

The wolf went straight to the castle like a person who

She managed to slip out so slyly that the King
did not see where she was gone. (Page 224)

Then the dragon made a dart at the hunter,
but he swung his sword round and cut off
three of the beast's heads. (Page 254)

feared nobody, and, when he came into the Princess's chamber, he plucked at her clothes behind so that she looked round. The maiden knew the wolf by his necklace, and took him with her into her room, and said, " Dear wolf, what do you want? "

The beast replied, " My master who killed the dragon is here, and has sent me for some vegetables like those the King eats to-day."

Then she bade the cook prepare a dish of vegetables the same as the King's, and carry it to the inn door for the wolf, who took it of her and bore it in to his master. The hunter said, " See here, my host: now I have bread, meat and vegetables the same as the King's; but I will also have the same sweetmeats." Then he called to the bear, " Dear bear, go and fetch me some sweetmeats like those the King has for his dinner to-day, for you like sweet things." The bear rolled along up to the castle, while every one got out of his way; but, when he came to the guard, he pointed his gun at him, and would not let him pass into the royal apartments. The bear, however, got up on his hind legs, and gave the guard right and left a box on the ears with his paw, which knocked him down; and thereupon he went straight to the room of the Princess, and, getting behind her, growled slightly. She looked round, and perceived the bear, whom she took into her own chamber, and asked him what he came for. " My master who slew the dragon is here," said he, "and has sent me for some sweetmeats such as the King eats." The Princess let the sugar-baker be called, and bade him prepare sweetmeats like those the King had, and carry them for the bear to the inn. There the bear took charge of them; and, first licking off the sugar which had boiled over, he took them in to his master.

"See here, friend landlord," said the huntsman; "now I have bread, meat, vegetables and sweetmeats from the table of the King; but I mean also to drink his wine."

He called the lion, and said, "Dear lion, I should be glad to have a draught; go and fetch me some wine like that the King drinks."

The lion strode through the town, where all the people made way for him, and soon came to the castle, where the watchmen attempted to stop him at the gates; but, just giving a little bit of a roar, they were so frightened that they all ran away. He walked on to the royal apartments, and knocked with his tail at the door; and, when the Princess opened it, she was at first frightened to see a lion; but, soon recognising him by the gold snap of her necklace which he wore, she took him into her room, and asked, "Dear lion, what do you wish?"

The lion replied, "My master who killed the dragon is here, and has sent me to fetch him wine like that the

King drinks at his own table." The Princess summoned the butler, and told him to give the lion wine such as the King drank. But the lion said, "I will go down with you and see that I have the right." So he went with the butler; and, as they were come below, he was about to draw the ordinary wine, such as was drunk by the King's servants, but the lion cried, "Hold! I will first taste the wine"; and, drawing for himself half a cupful, he drank it, and said, "No! that is not the real wine." The butler looked at him askance, and went to draw from another cask which was made for the King's Marshal. Then the lion cried, "Hold! first I must taste"; and, drawing half a flagonful, he drank it off, and said, "This is better; but still not the right wine." At these words the butler put himself in a passion, and said, "What does such a stupid calf as you know about wine?" The lion gave him a blow behind the ear, so that he fell down upon the ground; and as soon as he came to himself he led the lion quite submissively into a peculiar little cellar where the King's wine was kept, of which no one ever dared to taste. But the lion, first drawing for himself half a cupful, tried the wine, and saying, "This must be the real stuff," bade the butler fill six bottles with it. When this was done they mounted the steps again, and as the lion came out of the cellar into the fresh air he reeled about, being a little elevated; so that the butler had to carry the wine basket for him to the inn, where the lion, taking it again in his mouth, carried it in to his master. The hunter called the landlord, and said, "See here; now I have bread, meat, vegetables, sweetmeats and wine, the very same as the King will himself eat to-day, and so I will make my dinner with my animals." They sat down and ate and drank away, for he gave the hare, the fox, the wolf, the bear and the lion their share of the good things, and was very happy, for he felt the King's daughter still loved him. When he had finished his meal he said to the landlord, "Now, as I have eaten and drunk the same things as the King, I will even go to the royal palace and marry the Princess."

The landlord said, "How can that be, for she is already betrothed, and to-day the wedding is to be celebrated!"

Then the hunter drew out the handkerchief which the King's daughter had given him on the dragon's mountain, and wherein the seven tongues of the dragon's seven heads were wrapped, and said, "This shall help me to do it."

The landlord looked at the handkerchief and said, "If I believe all that has been done, still I cannot believe that, and will wager my house and garden upon it."

Thereupon the huntsman took out a purse with a thousand gold pieces in it, and said, "I will bet you that against your house and garden."

Meantime the King asked his daughter, "What do all these wild beasts mean who have come to you to-day, and passed and repassed in and out of my castle?"

She replied, "I dare not tell you, but send and let the master of these beasts be fetched, and you will do well."

The King sent a servant to the inn to invite the strange man to come, and arrived just as the hunter had concluded his wager with the landlord. So he said, "See, mine host, the King even sends a servant to invite me to come, but I do not go yet." And to the servant he said, "I beg that the King will send me royal clothes, and a carriage with six horses, and servants to wait on me."

When the King heard this answer, he said to his daughter, "What shall I do?" "Do as he desires, and you will do well," she replied. So the King sent a suit of royal clothes, a carriage with six horses, and some servants to wait upon the man. As the hunter saw them coming, he said to the landlord, "See here, I am fetched just as I desired," and, putting on the royal clothes, he took the handkerchief with him and drove to the King. When the King saw him coming, he asked his daughter how he should receive him, and she said, "Go out to meet him, and you will do well." So the King met him and led him into the palace, the animals following. The King showed him a seat near himself and his daughter, and the Marshal sat upon the other side as the bridegroom. Now, against the walls was the seven-headed dragon placed, stuffed as if it were yet alive; and the King said, "The seven heads of that dragon were cut off by our Marshal, to whom this day I give my daughter in marriage."

Then the hunter rose up, and, opening the seven jaws of the dragon, asked where were the seven tongues. This frightened the Marshal, and he turned pale as death, but at last, not knowing what else to say, he stammered out, "Dragons have no tongues."

The hunter replied, "*Liars* should have none, but the dragon's tongues are the trophies of the dragon slayer"; and so saying he unwrapped the handkerchief, and there lay all seven, and he put one into each mouth of the monster, and they fitted exactly. Then he took the handkerchief upon which her name was marked and showed it to the maiden, and asked her to whom she had given it, and she replied, "To him who slew the dragon." Then he called his beasts, and taking from each the necklace, and from the lion the golden snap, he put them together, and showing them to the Princess too, asked to whom they belonged. The Princess said, "The necklace and the snap were mine, and I shared it among the animals who helped to conquer the dragon." Then the huntsman said, "When I was weary and rested after the fight, the Marshal came and cut off my head, and then took away the Princess, and gave out that it was he who had conquered the dragon. Now that he has lied, I show these tongues, this necklace and this handkerchief for proofs." And then he related how the beasts had cured him with a wonderful root, and that for a year he had wandered, and at last had come hither again, where he had discovered the deceit of the Marshal through the innkeeper's tale. Then the King asked his daughter, "Is it true that this man killed the dragon?"

"Yes," she replied, "it is true; for I dared not disclose the treachery of the Marshal, because he threatened me with instant death. But now it is known without my mention, and for this reason have I delayed the wedding a year and a day."

After these words the King ordered twelve councillors to be summoned who should judge the Marshal, and these condemned him to be torn in pieces by four oxen. So the Marshal was executed, and the King gave his daughter to the huntsman, and named him Stadtholder over all his kingdom. The wedding was celebrated with great joy, and the young King caused his father and foster-father to be brought to him, and loaded them with presents. He did not forget either the landlord, but bade him welcome, and said to him, "See you here, my host; I have married the daughter of the King, and thy house and garden are mine." The landlord said that was according to right; but the young King said, "It shall be according to mercy"; and he gave him back not only his house and garden, but also presented him with the thousand gold pieces he had wagered.

Now the young King and Queen were very happy, and lived together in contentment. He often went out hunting, because he delighted in it; and the faithful animals always accompanied him.

In the neighbourhood there was a forest which it was said was haunted, and that if one entered it he did not easily get out again. The young King, however, took a great fancy to hunt in it, and he let the old King have no peace till he consented to let him. Away then he rode with a great company; and, as he approached the forest, he saw a snow-white hind going into it; so telling his companions to await his return, he rode off among the trees, and only his faithful beasts accompanied him. The courtiers waited and waited till evening, but he did not return; so they rode home and told the young Queen that her husband had ridden into the forest after a white doe, and had not again come out. The news made her very anxious about him. He, however, had ridden farther and farther into the wood after the beautiful animal without catching it; and, when he thought it was within range of his gun, with one spring it got away, till at last it disappeared altogether. Then he remarked for the first time how deeply he had plunged into the thickets; and, taking his horn, he gave a blast, but there was no answer, for his people could not hear it. Presently night began to close in; and perceiving that he could not get home that day, he dismounted, and, making a fire, prepared to pass the night. While he sat by the fire, with his beasts lying near all around him, he thought he heard a human voice, but, on looking round, he could see nobody. Soon after he heard again a groan, as if from a box; and, looking up, he saw an old woman sitting upon the tree, who was groaning and crying, "Oh, oh, oh, how I do freeze!" He called out, "Come down and warm yourself if you freeze." But she said, "No; your beasts will bite me." He replied, "They will not harm you, my good lady, if you like to come down." But she was a witch, and said, "I will throw you down a twig, which if you beat upon their backs they will then do nothing to me." He did as was requested; and immediately they lay down quietly enough, for they were changed into stones. Now, when the old woman was safe from the animals, she sprang down, and, touching the King too with a twig, converted him also into a stone. Thereupon she laughed to herself, and buried him and his beasts in a grave where already were many more stones.

Meantime the young Queen was becoming more and more anxious and sad when her husband did not return;

and just then it happened that the other brother, who had travelled towards the east when they separated, came into the territory. He had been seeking and had found no service to enter, and was, therefore, travelling through the country, and making his animals dance for a living. Once he thought he would go and look at the knife which they had stuck in a tree at their separation, in order to see how his brother fared. When he looked at it, lo! his brother's side was half rusty and half bright! At this he was frightened, and thought his brother had fallen into some great misfortune; but he hoped yet to save him, for one half of the knife was bright. He therefore went with his beasts towards the west; and, as he came to the capital city, the watch went out to him, and asked if he should mention his arrival to his bride, for the young Queen had for two days been in great sorrow and distress at his absence, and feared he had been killed in the enchanted wood. The watchman thought certainly he was no one else than the young King, for he was so much like him, and had also the same wild beasts returning after him. The huntsman perceived he was speaking of his brother, and thought it was all for the best that he should give himself out as his brother, for so, perhaps, he might more easily save him. So he let himself be conducted by the watchman into the castle, and was there received with great joy, for the young Queen took him for her husband also, and asked him where he had stopped so long. He told her he had lost his way in a wood, and could not find his way out earlier.

For a couple of days he rested at home, but was always asking about the enchanted wood; and at last he said, "I must hunt there once more." The King and the young Queen tried to dissuade him, but he was resolved and went out with a great number of attendants. As soon as he got into the wood, it happened to him as to his brother: he saw a white hind, and told his people to wait his return where they were, while he hunted the wild animal, and immediately rode off, his beasts following his footsteps. But he could not catch the hind any more than his brother; and he went so deep into the wood that he had to pass the night there. As soon as he had made a fire, he heard some one groaning above him, and saying, "Oh, oh, oh, how I do freeze!" Then he looked up and there sat the same old witch in the tree, and he said to her, "If you freeze, old woman, why don't you come down and warm yourself?" She replied, "No, your beasts would bite me; but if you would beat them with a twig which I will throw down to you, they can do me no harm." When the hunter heard this, he doubted the old woman, and said to her, "I do not beat my beasts; so come down, or I will fetch you." But she called out, "What are you thinking of, you can do nothing to me?" He answered, "Come down, or I will shoot you." The old woman laughed, and said, "Shoot away! I am not afraid of your bullets!"

He knelt down and shot, but she was bullet proof; and, laughing till she yelled, called out, "You cannot catch me." However, the hunter knew a trick or two, and tearing three silver buttons from his coat, he loaded his gun with them; and, while he was ramming them down, the old witch threw herself from the tree with a loud shriek, for she was not proof against such shot. He placed his foot upon her neck, and said, "Old witch, if you do not tell me quickly where my brother is, I will tie your hands together, and throw you into the fire!"

She was in great anguish, begged for mercy, and said, "He lies with his beasts in a grave, turned into stone." Then he forced her to go with him, threatening her, and saying, "You old cat! now turn my brother and all the creatures which lie here into their proper forms, or I will throw you into the fire!"

The old witch took a twig, and changed the stones back to what they were; and immediately his brother and the beasts stood before the huntsman, as well as many merchants, workpeople, and shepherds who, delighted with their freedom, returned home; but the twin brothers, when they saw each other again, kissed and embraced, and were very glad. They seized the old witch, bound her, and laid her on the fire; and, when she was consumed, the forest itself disappeared, and all was clear and free from trees, so that one could see the royal palace three miles off.

Now the two brothers went together home; and on the way told each other their adventures. And when the younger one said he was lord over the whole land in place of the King, the other one said, "All that I was well aware of, for when I went into the city I was taken for you. And all kingly honour was paid to me, the young Queen even mistaking me for her true husband, and making me sit at her table, and sleep in her room." When the first one heard this, he became very angry, and so jealous and passionate that, drawing his sword, he cut off the head of his brother. But as soon as he had done so, and saw the red blood flowing from the dead body, he repented sorely, and said, "My brother has saved me, and I have killed him for so doing"; and he groaned pitifully. Just then the hare came, and offered to fetch the healing root, and then, running off, brought it just at the right time, so that the dead man was restored to life again, and not even the mark of the wound was to be seen.

After this adventure they went on, and the younger brother said, "You see that we have both got on royal robes, and have both the same beasts following us; we will, therefore, enter the city at opposite gates, and arrive from the two quarters the same time before the King."

So they separated; and at the same moment the watchman from each gate came to the King, and informed him that the young Prince with the beasts had returned from the hunt. The King said, "It is not possible, for your two gates are a mile asunder!" But in the meantime the two brothers had arrived in the castle yard, and began to mount the stairs. When they entered, the King said to his daughter, "Tell me which is your husband, for one appears to me the same as the other, and I cannot tell." The Princess was in great trouble, and could not tell which was which: but at last she bethought herself of the necklace which she had given to the beasts, and she looked and found on one of the lions her golden snap, and then she cried exultingly, "He to whom this lion belongs is my rightful husband." Then the young King laughed and said, "Yes, that is right"; and they sat down together at table, and ate and drank and were merry. At night when the young King went to bed, his wife asked him why he had placed on the two previous nights a sword in the bed, for she thought it was to kill her. Then the young King knew how faithful his brother had been.